Dirty to the Grave

KN

Dirty to the Grave

Karen Williams

www.urbanbooks.net

Urban Books, LLC
78 East Industry Court
Deer Park, NY 11729

Dirty to the Grave ©copyright 2010 Karen Williams

ISBN 13: 978-1-60162-269-3
ISBN 10: 1-60162-269-4

First Printing April 2010
Printed in the United States of America

10 9 8 7 6 5 4 3 2 1

This is a work of fiction. Any references or similarities to actual events, real people, living, or dead, or to real locales are intended to give the novel a sense of reality. Any similarity in other names, characters, places, and incidents is entirely coincidental.

Distributed by Kensington Publishing Corp.
Submit Wholesale Orders to:
Kensington Publishing Corp.
C/O Penguin Group (USA) Inc.
Attention: Order Processing
405 Murray Hill Parkway
East Rutherford, NJ 07073-2316
Phone: 1-800-526-0275
Fax: 1-800-227-9604

Dedication

This novel is dedicated to my shining star.
Bralynn Bryce Graham born July 23, 2009.
I feel so blessed.

Acknowledgments

      I have never in my life felt the challenges in writing as I did with this novel. For starters, I hand wrote the whole thing because I was having some serious back problems and couldn't sit at my computer. And for over a year procrastinated on typing the story. I went from trying to pay someone to type it (but the handwriting was too sloppy) to snatching my sister's laptop and giving myself a month to type it. *Swipper, no swipe Crystal.* And for over a year that laptop and the notebook sat on my coffee table. Eventually I managed to get it done. I am so happy to bring you guys this story. But it was not easy between pregnancy, swollen feet and ankles, labor, feeding, burping, and changing my newborn son, the story is done.

      Okay, as usual I have to thank my crazy mother and my sister Crystal for their support. You both are there for me when the wave is rough and when it is smooth. And to my daughter Adara, you have experienced so much with me. And you make a very good older sister. J Love you always. And I can't forget the usual suspects, my nieces Mikayla and Madison. My nephew Omari. My cousins Donnie, Jabrez, Devin, and Mu-Mu. My goddaughter La'naya. Hey, to Tammy, Shauntae, Ray, Eric, Christina, and Michael. Ms. Graham, you are like a second mom to me. Thanks for always taking the time to listen and offer me pure wisdom.

To my friends, Lenzie I don't even know what to say. But you finally read the book, two years later! I know you got me though. And as usual I'm still laughing. Kimberly thanks for everything. I am really fortunate to have you as a friend. Many blessings to Linda for always being there for me. If you need anything from a lock fixed to aromatherapy Linda is the go-to-person and you are now a part of the family. Now I like calling you Roxie but I promised I'd put your full name here. So thanks Roxetta for being such a good friend. You are hard to come by. I am glad I can count on you as being my girl. Tracy I can't begin to thank you for all you have done for me. You were there during my darkest time. God brought you into my life. Christina do you know how long I wanted us to reconnect? It feels like no time has passed between us. I love you Cheryl, and there is so much beauty in you. I love you Christina Talamontes! I need some of your wisdom. Hey Carla, we will always have that GSHU bond. I miss working with you. Thanks to, Misty, Sewiaa, Ronisha RIP , Tina, Valerie Hoyt, Tara, Pearlean, Maxine, Jennifer, Barbara, Henrietta, Candis, VI, Phillipo, Latonya, Tymisha, Leigh, and Vanilla. Hey, Dena! And man do I miss having lunch with the one and only Ivonne Gayner from the dirty south! Hey, Sandra. Hey, Marilyn. Please behave. Hey, Ivy, Daphne, and Lydia! I can't forget Mrs. Pope!

I also want to thank my fans for all your support. I'll keep writing for you guys!

To Terry, thanks for showing me what it's like to be loved, valued, and treasured. And for the beautiful gift you gave me. I will always love you.

Chapter 1

Goldie

I loved chillin' with my girls 'cause, wherever we went, from Bistro 880 to The Century Club, we were the baddest bitches in there. Today we were at the Hollywood Casino in Inglewood. How Red got these tickets to see Katt Williams was beyond me, but I didn't really care. I was happy to be there.

I was wearing a tight-ass hot-pink dress I got at Fashion Trend in Lakewood with some stillettos I caught on sale right next door at Rainbow. Them bitches was a half-size too small, but I was killing the hell out of my dress and them heels.

Red had on booty shorts, a sexy gold silk top, and knee-high boots.

I almost fell over laughing when Cha's son said to Cha, "Mama, she looks like the Catwoman!"

And Cha had on a pair of simple blue low-rise jeans, a black tube top, and leather boots.

See, we were high-class with low-class clothes, whereas the other bitches there were low-class with high-class clothes. Hell, we didn't have that high-class shit, but the bottom line is this: If you're fly by nature, it doesn't matter that you don't rock name-brand items. And we had knockout bodies, so whatever we put on looked good on us.

We were just trying to survive in the world, living in a

low-income building, swiping EBT cards, getting money out
of dudes, and a little hustling here and there. What the fuck
we know about Christian Dior or Dolce & Gabbana, except
what we saw on TV? And, yeah, what we saw here? But that
still didn't stop our shine.

It was comedy night, and Katt Williams' little permed-
out-ass had us cracking up. And, of course, like all comedians
who run out of jokes, he ended up turning to the crowd and
clowning.

"Who you think he gonna get at?" Cha asked Red and
me.

"Probably them raggedy bitches over there," Red said,
pointing.

I chuckled and put my head down, and sure enough,
that's where he went. To the table closest to the stage. But
having the table closest to the stage didn't mean shit. All it really meant was that the bitches got there earlier than anybody,
or one of them got their flirt on and "bogarted" the whole
table. Simple. It was eight of them bitches all huddled at that
little-ass table.

The spotlight hit the table as he spoke.

"Damn! Y'all drinking Moët and shit," he said in his
squeaky-ass voice. "Gotdamn! Can I sit with y'all muthafuckas?"

One chick laughed out loud, put her glass in the air,
and shouted loudly, "Ballin'!"

Red shook her head. "Them bitches ain't ballin'. We
the ballin' bitches."

Me and Cha was cracking up 'cause while we wasn't
balling, we didn't look raggedly like them. It never amazes me
how tacky bitches can be.

At our table we had two bottles of Moët, a bottle of

Dom Pérignon, all courtesy of niggas sending us shit all night, not to mention the bottle of Cristal we politely sent back. We just didn't drink that shit.

Red repeated more loudly, "Them bitches ain't ballin'!"

You know Red. She couldn't have no chick upstaging her, no matter what.

Cha glanced at me as I tried to hold my giggle in, the spotlight **was** now on us.

"In fact," Red said, "ain't none of these bitches in here flyer than we are!"

Murmurs and laughs came from the crowd.

The eight chicks Red got at kept their heads down. They probably knew who we were, but the others, I couldn't be sure.

At another table, one chickenhead, one weavealicious, and a red bone redder than my girl Red shot looks our way, clearly mean-mugging us.

"Oh, shit!" Katt said. "Now y'all done started something. It's about to go down. I just wanna see a couple nipples and bootyholes."

The crowd laughed, and the girls kept mean-mugging us.

Red Bone asked Red, "Whatchu say?"

Red stood and planted her hand on her hips. "You heard. I said, 'Ain't no bitches in here ballin.' What?" She spread her arms wide.

Weavealicious yelled, "We wasn't even in that shit, but since you wanna make public announcements—Who the fuck you callin' bitches? 'Cause I ain't nobody's bitch!"

Cha lowered her gaze, as I sipped on my third glass of Moët.

"Y'all," Red said.

All of a sudden, a Hpnotiq bottle came flying at us.

With that, we headed over to them hoes' table. Red grabbed Red Bone, and Cha went after Chickenhead.

I smacked Weavealicious, and served that bitch blow after blow, holding onto her weave for leverage. She leaned forward and swung but couldn't get a lick in. I bashed her head in a few good times before she slid to the floor.

I spied Cha roughing up Chickenhead, and Red, as usual, was getting her ass whipped. Why? After all that shit she talked? Simple. She was my girl, but the bitch couldn't fight.

I rushed over to where she was and used my closed fist to sock Red Bone in the side of her neck, sending her crashing into her table.

"Yeah, bitch!" Red yelled when the girl hit the floor. She crouched low and pummeled Red Bone in the face.

That's when I felt myself being lifted in the air and thrown against a beefy chest. It was a bouncer. I looked up and saw the same being done to Cha and Red.

The bouncer carrying me whispered, "Baby, let me get your number."

I laughed and struggled in his beefy arms.

They didn't let us go until we were outside the club, where they dumped us on the concrete. The one who dumped me copped a little feel of my round ass first.

"Fuck y'all rent-a-cops!" Red yelled.

Too out of breath to even respond to the dude that rubbed on me, I placed my hand on my chest. I looked at Cha staring at Red and read her thoughts. I yelled, "Bitch, we can't take yo' trouble-starting ass nowhere!"

Red tilted her head back and burst out laughing.

Then we were all laughing on the concrete. Yep, from time to time, that was our "get-down."

Chapter 2

Red

"Clean that shit, little monkey." I was four years old when I understood the difference between white folks and black folks. I knew blacks were inferior, dumb, lazy, ugly, and a total waste to the planet. I knew whites were smart, elite, talented, and successful. But the only problem was, I was black. Well, half-black anyway.

My daddy was black, but ask me if I ever seen him. I ain't never seen him. He had a wife and kids, so my mama was just his sideline ho.

Then she got slick and got knocked up with me, thinking he was gonna leave his wife. Wrong. My pops shook the spot, leaving her to raise me.

My mama happened to be white, and if you didn't figure that out, you a dumb ass. And that same fair skin, freckles, and long hair she had, I had too.

I was five years old and had just got tested for school. They said I was smart, so they wanted me to skip kindergarten and go straight to first grade.

The principal told my mama, "You should be very proud of your child."

But Miss Mabel was pissed. Wasn't nothing happy 'bout her expression.

Walking three paces behind her, like she always had me do, I reached for her hand on the way home from school, and she jerked back. I don't know why I did that. Naw, I knew why I did it. When other parents picked up their kids, they hugged them and strolled hand in hand, and that's what I wanted.

"Nigger, don't touch me," she mumbled.

As soon as we made it to our house, she shoved me toward the backyard. I hated going out there 'cause Bopeep, our rottweiler, was out there.

"Mommy, no."

That got me a kick in my ass, and I fell back on the ground, screaming as I went down.

My mama opened the gate and dragged me by my long red hair, until I was lying on the dirty grass and Bopeep was looking at me like he wanted to gobble me right up.

"Jigaboo, listen to me," my mama said, the sun in her face. "You are a nigger. That's all you are ever going to be. And you ain't smart. You dumb as shit. Bopeep over there got more smarts than you do. Monkey! So you wanna be cute at school and show off, then you can stay on out here with Bopeep. You can eat, shit, and sleep with him 'till you learn your place in the world."

I crawled into a corner and sat there. I thought my mama was messing around at first, but then the sun started fading. I'd been holding my pee-pee in, until finally it gave out on me, and I peed on myself, soaking my stockinged legs.

The sun turned a different color. Then it disappeared. That's when I seen my mama. I was hungry and thirsty. I thought she was gonna call me in the house, but she brought a pot and turned it over, so the contents, which looked like scraps of chicken bones, rice, and peas, fell to the dirt-covered ground.

Bopeep dove right in it.

"I'm hungry, Mama."

"Then get your black ass down there and eat with Bopeep!"

I closed my eyes and cried as the door closed.

When it was nightfall, I knocked on my mama's back door. "Please let me in, Mama. I'm scared."

I knocked over and over until my knuckles were red and aching, but Mama didn't answer. I sobbed and went back to the corner I had abandoned earlier. I had no choice but to sleep.

Splash!

I blinked and wiped the cold water from my eyes and nose.

"Wash up with the dog, nigger face."

I scrubbed my eyes, whining and calling my mom's name. I crawled on the porch steps and grabbed her ankle.

She kicked me in the forehead. "Nigger, get off me!"

I fell back hard on Bopeep, making him growl at me. I ignored the pain in my side and the knot on my head and snatched myself up and rushed to the other side of the backyard, where I stayed in my stinky clothes. The piss had dried on me, but I remember the wetness made the dirt cling to me. Now that too had dried up and down my legs like I was in a mud fight and was itching me and attracting flies.

She didn't feed me, and me being so hungry, my stomach wouldn't stop growling. I snuck over to Bopeep's side while he was sleeping and snatched up some of his Kibbles 'n Bits. Then I crawled back over to my side.

I popped one in my mouth and chewed slowly. I gagged at first when the taste hit my mouth, but I was able to get the second and third down.

"Well, looka here."

I froze and stared up at my mother slowly.

She burst out laughing. "All this time I been calling you a monkey 'cause that's what all you niggers are, but I was wrong about you. You a damn dog, nigger girl, munching on Kibbles 'n Bits."

I dropped the dog food from my hands.

"And I brought you some dinner, but"—She bit her bottom lip like she was in serious thought—" "since you like dog food so much, your ass can eat it, and I'll give this to Bopeep."

I watched horrified as she poured out the food on the ground near Bopeep. Then she walked back over to me and poured some from the bag of dog food on the ground next to my feet.

"Mommy."

"No mommy nothing. Your black ass needs to be humbled. You need to learn your place—That's beneath the whites. That's y'all problem anyway." She left me out there again.

Later that night I heard crackling and crunching of leaves. It made me pant nervously, made my heart beat faster.

When I opened my eyes, I saw a big ol' rat my teacher at school said was called an opossum, cousin to the rat. Up close, it looked like a giant rat nibbling on the remainder of the Kibbles 'n Bits I couldn't manage to get down. He didn't care that I was half a feet away from him. He just kept on eating. I held my breath in, as he crunched and crunched.

My eyes passed over Bopeep's sleeping form. He was knocked out.

I prayed to God, even though Mama said He didn't

answer niggers' prayers because we were the offspring of Satan, the Antichrist.

One day as I was singing the hell out of "His Eye Is on
the Sparrow," she told me, "Your soul is as black as you are."

So I stopped believing in Him.

That night, though, I needed something to believe in,
so I prayed to God that the big rat didn't hurt me. My eyes
were closed shut, but my ears were not.

I heard Bopeep bark. The sounds the opossum was
making must have woken him. Bopeep rushed toward him,
and the opossum rose on his hind legs, showing his teeth and
his claws. He pounced on Bopeep, but he was no match. Bopeep went for his neck, got a good hold with his teeth, and was
tugging away. Blood was streaming from the opossum's neck,
but he tried to fight back by clawing Bopeep's face.

Bopeep wouldn't let go, his head moving side to side
as he dug deeper and deeper into the opossum's neck. The
opossum shuddered for a few moments then stopped moving.

I sobbed out of fear and from seeing all that blood.
Then Bopeep went back to his spot and fell asleep like nothing had happened.

I shivered and cried, calling out my mama's name,
but she wouldn't answer. When Bopeep started barking at
me, I shut up and quietly cried myself to sleep.

The next day, I felt myself being carried. I didn't bother opening my eyes 'cause I knew it was my mama. Maybe
she had forgiven me for yesterday, and was going to wash me
up and let me get in my own bed finally, so I didn't bother
opening my eyes or fussing. I was still half asleep when I felt
her peeling my clothes off. My mama carried me to the tub.

It felt good to have her holding me like that. Maybe she really did love me. I loved her. When my naked body started to burn, I screamed and popped my eyes open. Before I could move, my mother held me down in our tub. I was laying on a big trash bag that was inside on the tub and she was pouring stuff on me. One I already knew how to spell was bleach. I knew what it was 'cause it had a strong smell and my mama cleaned with it. The other smelled really bad and started with a-m-o. Then she began pouring that one on me. "Mama, no!" I screamed and rose from the tub. She shoved me back down with all her might. "Get your black ass back in here. You need to be cleansed." She yanked me back by my head and poured the stuff in my hair. I closed my eyes as it spilled down my face. I was screaming for my life, but the more I moved, the more blows I got. She spat in my face and yelled, "You fucking nigger!" I cried and screamed, begging her to stop, but she poured bottle after bottle on me, from my head to my feet, until the tub was filled with all those bottles of stuff. Then she took the pad she scrubbed the pots with in the kitchen and began scrubbing my body with it. I was on my back and had no way of stopping her 'cause she was straddling the tub and had both of her feet planted on my chest. "You're dirty. You need to be cleansed of all that sin that comes with being colored!" she yelled. Soon I became too weak to fight as the pad was shredding my skin, leaving it raw, and the liquids were burning those areas even more. I just gave up and let her put Ajax on me and scrub me until she was convinced I was cleansed, nearly passing out.

Chapter 3

Red

Thirteen Years Later

"Nigger, are you going to bring me the soup or not?"

"I'm coming, Mama," I yelled as I cradled some chicken broth and a cup of hot tea in my hands and carried it up to her room. That was all my mama could manage to hold down ever since she caught the stomach flu. I had it the week before she did, and she made me sleep in the backyard until I was better. But still she got it, and I been taking care of her ever since.

The first time she threw up, she took some Listerine and doused my eyes with it. "You fucking niggers with your viruses. Next thing you know, thanks to your black ass, I'll have AIDS."

Before I could even open the door, I heard, "Knock first, monkey!"

I placed the cup of tea and the bowl of broth in my forearm and knocked quickly before it could fall.

"Come in, tar baby."

I opened the door and walked over to my mother, hidden under four blankets and surrounded by about eight pillows.

"Are you gonna stand there or bring it over here, nigger?"

I walked over to her and sat the soup and tea on her nightstand. I stood and watched her drink the tea, making sure she did.

She slurped it in three gulps then sat it back down and looked at me. "Get the fuck out my room, jigaboo!"

I walked out of the room and into my own.

I quickly stripped down and eyed myself in the mirror, admiring my curves. I was now seventeen, soon to be eighteen.

I jumped under my covers and played with my pussy, getting it ready for my neighbor's son Deandre.

Ten minutes later, he was sneaking in the room.

I looked up into his face. Peanut butter skin, green eyes, pouty pink lips. But ten times more retarded than fucking Forrest Gump. "Come on," I said, throwing the covers off my naked body.

His eyes got buck, and within seconds he was naked and on top of me plunging his dick into me. Retarded yes. Virgin no. A few women on our street had their way with his Gump ass.

While he wasn't bad to look at, I had to shield my face 'cause slobber continued to pour from his mouth and he was making weird sounds. Once I felt him bust into me, I pulled away from him as he lay back on my bed trying to catch his breath.

"I I I let . . . levvvv. Leave now?" he asked. It took his slow ass damn near five minutes to get that question out.

"Naw. Chill. I'll be right back with a soda," I lied.

I tiptoed down to my mother's room and opened the door. I found her ass 'sleep, knocked out on her back and still covered by blankets.

I went toward her bed, grabbed one of the pillows that fell on the floor, and straddled her body, placing the pillow firmly over her face. She was so knocked out, at first she didn't realize I had taken away her air.

When she finally did, I used all my weight to press down on her face. She struggled, but the weight of my body was too much for her to throw me off. I pressed and pressed, and she struggled and struggled, until her arms lay limp at her sides and she couldn't really struggle no more.

The bitch was dead.

I pulled the pillow from her face and saw her mouth open, her blue eyes bloodshot and wide. I shook my head at her. "Stop fucking looking at me!" I yelled.

I commenced to beating her ass, punching her in her mouth over and over, 'till some loose teeth started flying. Then I wrapped my hands around her neck and started kneeing her in the stomach and slapping her across her face. I yanked strands of her thinning gray hair out.

I grabbed her letter-opener off her nightstand and hard as I could, stabbed her in the left eye. Then I pulled it out and did the same to her right. I backed away from the bed. "Now you straight, bitch." I took a bow.

I pulled one of her dresses out of the closet, took the curved end of the wire hanger, and stuck it up my pussy. I scratched my flesh until I started bleeding inside, all the while grunting at the pain. Then I put four scratches on my face and two on my neck.

I grabbed my neck and held it for thirty seconds, until it was red. I was "shit color," so I bruised easily. Then I reached for her phone and dialed 9-1-1.

As soon as they picked up, I screamed, "Help! I've been raped, and they killed my mama!"

Chapter 4

Cha

I wouldn't say I had the perfect life. Well, I mean, who could? But, for a girl from the hood, it was as good as it could get. I was twenty-three years old and never had a mom or dad. One of them sisters that left their baby at a firehouse, yeah, one of them was my mama. Only thing was, she didn't leave me at the firehouse. It was like out of one of those movies. She left me in a dumpster, and I stayed in a group home until I was eighteen.

Soon after I got out, I was lucky enough to meet Onyx, who was a little older than me, and a major "slanger" in Cali. He took me in and showed me what consensual sex was all about. Prior to him, from the time I sprouted breasts and my booty poked out, I was forced to give myself away to not only dudes in the group home, but also the director.

Onyx showed me what love felt like too, and despite his rep, he gave me real love. Healthy love.

Two years later, he gave me something even more precious, a bouncing baby boy. Little Omari was just as black as Onyx and had some long kitty-cat lashes and a heart-shaped face.

I knew what people always said about thugs, that they no-good, thieving, violent cheaters, but not my Onyx. Like

I said, he was the sweetest, kindest man I'd ever known. He went out and did his hustle thang and came back home and lay his head right on my lap. And on Saturdays he took Omari to the park, so I could hang with my girls, Red and Goldie.

But I didn't hang out too much. Being with my family was more important. I lived for it, and for a while, I had it. Then one day it was viciously snatched away from me.

December 2005

I was curled up on the couch with little Omari and Onyx watching *Shrek*. Omari was in my lap, and Onyx was massaging my feet. Just then, the phone rang.

"Excuse me, baby." Onyx rose and gently lay my legs on the couch.

I knew what the conversation would be like. It would be either Big Rob, Cornbread, or Trigger. They'd say, "Man, we partying, and we got some bitches with us. You coming?"

And Onyx would reply, "Naw, I'm chilling with my seed and my woman, fellas. See y'all on the block." And he'd always come right back to the couch, put my legs back on his lap, and go right back to rubbing them.

I knew his boys heckled him and called him soft, but Onyx didn't give a damn. We knew what he dealt with them fools for—to afford us a better life.

"Onyx, you sure you don't want to go hang with them on Broadway? Or to that club you like, Coco Cubana?"

His hold on me tightened. "Come on, baby. Where I am now is exactly where I wanna be."

"But you know if—"

He leaned over and kissed me. "I know, babe. That shit will never be me. I deal with them clowns for business, and that only."

I smiled and noticed that Omari had dozed.

"I got him." Onyx stood up and carried him to his room.

I turned the TV off and stretched.

The next thing I know, Onyx scooped me up and carried me into our room, lay me on the bed, and got me ready for the mind-blowing sex he was always sure to give me.

His kisses were always gentle at first, washing away all the men that stole kisses from me all through my adolescence. Onyx was the only man I ever freely gave my love to, because all the others before him took it.

Then, like clockwork, my baby held on to me for dear life.

See, that's how it was. In a couple of hours he would hit the block again with Big Rob, Cornbread, and Trigger. And there was always a possibility that he wouldn't come back, that the streets would claim him, so I had to make the best of every moment.

But the more work my baby put in, the steeper it became with each passing day, as he kept pushing more and more weight every time. For us. We already had forty Gs saved, but Onyx wanted to put twenty-five more with that before we moved to the South and opened up a business.

He wanted me to get a degree. I was always scared to tell him I was too dumb to go to college, but I loved that he thought I was smart. He was the only one who did, so I kept quiet.

Onyx was good with electronics. That boy could fix any and everything, so he wanted to open up a little shop, fix broken TVs and whatnot. Maybe, even install stereos and TVs in cars, which he knew how to do too.

We had it all planned. It was just a matter of him moving weight and me waiting and holding it down at home.

***

It was a Thursday night, the day I always seemed to have bad luck. I always overslept, couldn't get breakfast right, or finish my chores around the house. And, boy, if Omari picked any day to get into stuff, it would be a Thursday. But this Thursday got so much better when Onyx walked through the door.

I started taking the pieces of chicken out of the pan and put them onto a pan lined with paper towels. I felt bad because I wanted to be done by the time he got there. But I couldn't blame it on it being unlucky Thursday. My baby was just early.

"I'm done."

I checked the casserole made out of potatoes, onions, bell peppers, and cheese. I jumped when Onyx smacked me on my ass. "Hey, baby."

"Cha, did you hear what I said?"

"No." I went over to the stereo and turned the volume down on Alicia Keys "Troubles."

"I'm done."

He was playing, I thought, but it still didn't stop my mouth from gaping. "What?"

"You heard me. I'm done." He smiled and bit at his bottom lip.

"Say it again, baby!"

He grabbed me around my waist and snatched me away from the stove as chicken started popping like crazy. I didn't care; it could have burnt me, and I wouldn't have cared. But that was Onyx, always looking out for me.

He looked down at me. "Like I was saying, I'm out the game now."

I was getting excited. "What does that mean, Onyx?" I mean, I knew, but I guess I needed confirmation.

He stroked my face with his fingers. "It means that I'm not gonna be on the block ever again, baby. We can do what we been planning to do, and that's get the fuck out of the projects and out of Cali!"

As I laughed and hugged my baby close, Omari tugged at my shirt.

"Boy, why you in this kitchen? I told you to clean up them toys."

My little three-year-old looked at me like I was crazy.

Onyx chuckled at him and uttered the magic words. "Come on, boy. Let's get into some Xbox."

Omari ran out of the kitchen. Toddler or not he loved video games thanks to his daddy.

Onyx followed after him. "We'll talk about it later, baby." He winked at me and whispered, "In bed." Then he came back to grab a wing from the pan on the stove and kept tossing it in the air from the heat and went back to the living room.

I put my head down and blushed. We had been together four years, and he still managed to give me butterflies.

I went to the oven to check on the casserole. The cheese was bubbling. All I had to do was open a can of string beans, cook them, and that would be dinner.

I may have been a young mom, but I made sure my son ate healthy meals, fruits, vegetables, and that he took his vitamins.

Over the loud video game, I heard Onyx yell, "Come on, boy. You gotta do better than that!"

I chuckled and walked over to the cupboard for some string beans. I stood on my toes and sifted through cans of corn, peas, canned tuna, and oysters, hoping we had some string beans I could throw into a pot of onions with maybe a little sausage. I pushed aside some applesauce and found a can of string beans.

I turned back around to see how far they had gotten on the game, and the image before me caused me to drop the string beans on the floor, making a loud thud. My hands rushed to cover my mouth at what I was seeing. My son and my man were seated on the couch, and three men were facing me, one with a Glock, one with a pistol, and one with a .30-caliber pointed at my family.

I even blinked a couple of times, but it was still happening in my living room.

"That's Daddy's friends!" Omari shouted.

They were indeed men we knew—Big Rob, Cornbread, and Trigger, the niggas Onyx slang with on the block.

Before I could make a move, one of them said to me, "Get the boy, bitch, or we will heat him up too."

Onyx, never taking his eyes off the dudes, said, "Baby, get Omari."

Rushing over, I stumbled and fell. I crawled to my son and grabbed him without even getting up, and scooted back into the kitchen.

They started firing, and I started screaming, shielding my son and looking on horrified as the bullets pierced into the love of my life.

I couldn't do anything for Onyx, Omari, or myself. Nothing for Omari's screams at what he was seeing. He shook as I shook, and screamed as I screamed.

Once the love of my life was gone, the back of his head blown off, Trigger came at me with his gun drawn. "Move, bitch, or I'm blowing you and that punk-bitch son away, and y'all be in la-la land just like his punk-ass daddy." Trigger was Omari's godfather, and the one closest to Onyx.

I couldn't stop shaking. I wanted to rush towards Onyx. Maybe he was still breathing. Omari was screaming for his daddy, and each time he said daddy, his voice got louder.

The gun clicked, and Trigger slapped me in my face with it. I almost lost my balance on impact. Almost. I tasted my blood.

"Shut him up!"

I hugged Omari. "Baby, it's gonna be okay."

Omari was breathing hard, like he was gonna hyper-ventilate.

"Breath slowly, baby," I whispered.

The second hit from Trigger put a gash on my temple, and blood continued to stream from it. I ignored it and continued to rub Omari's back. He started hiccupping, and I tried my best to calm him. "Breathe, baby."

All the while, Trigger was eyeballing me in a way that Onyx, if he was alive, would've skinned his ass. His eyes were all over me, lushing on me. The man who killed my baby daddy. My man.

My skin was crawling. It's funny how you never know what a person would or wouldn't do, or even what they're really thinking about you all along.

Trigger slapped my titties with his gun. "Damn, baby! You thick. Umph." He grabbed one of my thighs and squeezed it, biting his bottom lip.

I tried to snatch away, but his fingers dug into my flesh.

He smirked at me.

I dropped my eyes to Omari, who had his head buried in my neck, and was gripping the top of my shirt in his small closed fist, his whole body shaking. I tried my best not to cry, so I could in some way calm him, but nothing I was doing was really working. My baby was terrified.

My heart slammed into my chest when more blood ran down the side of my face. I glanced over at Onyx's body again and moaned inside. I felt my heart flutter, felt the shit break.

Trigger yanked my son out of my arms.

"What are you doing?"

When my son screamed and kicked, Trigger backhanded him.

I lunged for the bastard, but he tossed my son to the side and cocked his gun at me when he saw me coming.

"Bitch, you make any more moves, I'll blast." He pursed his lips.

But his blasting didn't make a difference. I didn't care about dying.

Puzzled at the blank look on my face, Trigger pointed it at Omari.

"No!"

He lowered it, and grabbed my ankle, pulling me toward him.

"Omari, keep your eyes closed, baby . . . please."

I only heard the sound of a zipper. Mine. Then he was prodding with his fingers.

I kept my eyes closed. I wanted to claw this bastard's fucking face. I mean, here he was with the blood of the love of my life on his shirt, and he was sticking those same fingers that pulled the trigger into me!

"Damn, you fine! I always thought you was sexy, Cha."

I could hear stuff being tossed around as Big Rob and Cornbread rummaged through the apartment. *They killed Onyx for money?*

Trigger's zipper was next.

God, get me out of this . . . please!

He grabbed my hair. At first his hands slipped because I had short hair. Then he gripped my neck, trying to pull my face down on his dick.

I pulled my lips in and held my breath.

"Bone it, ho."

"Please . . . not in front of my son!"

Wham! He slammed his gun on the back of my neck.

I had no choice but to rest my throbbing head and neck in his lap. I felt the tip of his penis rub against my cheek. I cringed inside in a way I never had. I wanted to gag. I heard my baby's sniffling. My heart was dead.

"We got it."

My head shot up.

"What the fuck you doing?" Big Rob and Cornbread were back in my living room, Cornbread leading the pack with a black duffel bag. They stared at us on the floor in surprise.

"Move, bitch!" Trigger shoved me off of him.

I crawled away and reached for Omari and hugged him to my chest.

"Damn!" Trigger shouted. "I sure wanted to stick my dick in that."

I watched in silence, screaming inside, as the same dudes Onyx had slanged with and called up every week to chill with acted like it wasn't shit that they'd robbed and murdered their supposed boy.

Big Rob shrugged. "Shit! Go ahead. Don't nobody give a fuck. This bitch was keeping Onyx on lockdown anyway."

"No!" I screamed.

Before I could get away, Big Rob came toward me and snatched Omari out of my arms. Meanwhile, Cornbread had already dropped the duffel bag and his pants, and was making his way toward me, his dick hanging.

While Trigger pulled my pants down, Big Rob carried Omari to the couch and said, "Come on, little man. Let's get into this Xbox!"

When I screamed, Trigger put a huge hand over my mouth. I was forced to get on my knees, and Trigger rammed me from behind, while Cornbread shoved his dick in my mouth.

Before I could even pray that Omari didn't see this, I looked between Cornbread's legs and saw Big Rob playing the same game that Onyx was playing earlier. Only, Omari wasn't playing, but was on his knees looking over the edge of the couch at what was happening to me.

The pressure of Trigger stabbing into me from behind was so intense, I felt like I was going to pass out. And Cornbread was gripping my head so tight, his nails were sinking into my skin, and he was shoving his dick in my mouth just as hard as Trigger was shoving his dick into my pussy.

I gave up the fight and just prayed it would be over soon.

Just as Trigger and Cornbread finished, Big Rob stood from the couch and took Cornbread's spot, and Cornbread took Trigger's spot, and it started all over again.

Chapter 5

Goldie

I didn't love nobody more than I loved my mama. And I had two good reasons. For starters, my mama was all I'd ever had, since my daddy, who was the love of her life and a highway patrolman, passed away when I was six.

The second reason I loved my mom more than anybody else was because she was the best type of mama to have. At five feet four, she was strong as hell. Her dreads, which she started growing shortly after marrying my daddy, were damn near as tall as she was. She was brown-skinned, and I inherited that beautiful hue. And she had these eyes the color of cinnamon. That's why she said her mama named her Cinnamon.

My mom taught political studies and race relations at UCLA. On weeknights she would sneak me in class, and I would watch her lecture the students. My mama had this way with words. She would stand her short-ass up on her podium like she was six feet and dare someone to fall asleep in her class or start talking. If I even heard a whisper from someone, I would give them a mean look, or I would alert my mama to the talkers. She would move her arms and talk with so much confidence. And if she'd given me permission to curse, I would've said, "Yeah, this black woman knows her shit."

We would walk down the campus on our way home,

and I would always ask her, "Mama, where do you think my choices will lead me?" It was something she'd asked the freshmen in her class.

She pierced me with a look, hardening up her soft eyes. "Your choices better be to carry yourself as a young lady, showing your manners, self-confidence, stature, and finishing school. And by school, young lady, I mean college!"

Yep, my mama had been telling me since I was freakin' three that college wasn't an option. I had to go.

She looked at me and my calculating expression and laughed.

"What you laughing at, Mommy?"

"You. Because you look like your father when you make that face."

Talk of dad always depressed her and me. I wrapped my arm around her because I saw her tearing up. She was still grieving over his death. I hadn't gotten over his death either, just always pushed it to the back of my mind.

The day I lost my mom was a day that plagues me to this day. I was twelve then. We were driving back from UCLA, listening to music from that doggone Stephanie Mills "The Power of Love" when police pulled us over.

"Lord." My mama smacked her teeth and peered in her rearview mirror at the flashing lights, which made my heart speed up. She slowed her speed, put on her signal, and slipped over slowly to the right. Once she stopped, she placed the car in park and turned off the ignition.

The officer's lights were blinding the hell out of both of us. Suddenly a man's face was in the window of my mother's car, on her side.

"Hello."

"Hello, officer," she said calmly.

"Wild night?" He raised his flashlight into the car and shined it on us.

"Officer, can you remove that light out of my child's face, please?"

The comment looked like it offended him. He ignored her and shined it harder. "Ma'am, do you have any idea how fast you were going?"

"Yes. Twenty-three miles per hour in a thirty-mile-per-hour zone."

"Ma'am, are you getting smart with me?"

"No, not at all. Just stating the truth, officer."

He didn't like that. I could tell. His jaw twitched. "Where are you coming from?"

"UCLA."

"You look old to be a student."

"That's because I'm not. I teach there." My mother didn't drop her gaze as he continued to stare at her.

He smirked like she was lying. "Well, what are you doing over here?"

By "here," the officer was referring to the city of Ladera Heights, where we lived in a two-story home.

"We live here."

He looked at my mom and smirked. "Be serious, ma'am. I know y'all don't live over here. Now what are you really doing? Your baby daddy a dopeman and you came to do a pickup?"

My mom stayed calm. "This conversation is not apprioprate, officer, and especially in front of my daughter. Can I please have your badge number?"

"Gal, step out of the car."

"Why—"

Before she could finish, he opened her door and pulled her out. I screamed when she fell on the concrete.

"Godiva, stay in the car!" she ordered.

Before she could stand to her feet, the cop yanked her up again and pulled her to his car. "If it's one thing I hate, it's an uppity, educated nigger."

Against my mother's wishes, I slipped out of my side of the car and crept out, as his back was to me. In my hands was the stun gun my mother always had hidden under her seat. I tiptoed to the edge of the car and watched the cop frisk her.

"You don't have the right to touch me! I demand a female to search me, officer. I know what my rights are."

I cringed inside as he grabbed my mother's ass then both her breasts. Then, in one quick motion, his hand went underneath her skirt, and I heard my mother's panties tear.

She screamed and pushed him. "Don't touch me, you bastard!" She took a few steps back, to get away from him.

He pulled his gun out and aimed it at her. Rushed her again, put the gun to her temple. "Nigger, you move, I'll kill you." He spun her around, shoved her up against his squad car, and raised her skirt.

That's when I screamed and went after the officer, stun gun in hand.

It startled him, and he aimed his gun at me.

Then a shot rang out, and smoke clouded the air.

He panicked and fired again. "Put down that gun, nigger!" he yelled at me.

"Officer, please . . . it's not a gun!" my mom yelled, terrified. "Don't shoot my baby!"

He ignored her and repeated. "Put down that gun!"

I shook my head and tried to say what my mom said, but the words wouldn't come out, and having a gun pointed at me, all I could do was pee in my pants.

He fired at me again.

I ducked, screamed, and watched my mom try to tackle the gun from out of his arms before he fired another shot in my direction.

"Don't kill my baby!"

Two more were fired, and they still struggled, her hands over his as his were over the gun. He yanked back, but she held on, and they both fell into the police car.

"Mama!"

Another shot fired, and my mom froze. She fell against the officer and then slowly slid to the ground.

Yep, that's how I lost my mama.

Chapter 6

Red

I split my blunt open and put my Indigo weed up in it. Then I licked the outside, rolled it back up real good, and lit that shit. I took a long-ass drag and passed it to Goldie, who gave me an annoyed look before taking it out of my hand and having a few puffs.

After a few moments of silence, she yelled out, "This bitch!" and smiled.

Cha chuckled. "Red, all I'm gonna say is that your behind is crazy!"

I got back the blunt from Goldie and tried to pass it to Cha, but she waved it away. I knew she wasn't gonna take it, but I still always tried.

I puffed again and ignored her holier-than-thou ass. "Them bitches needed to be put in their place."

"Let you tell it." Goldie snatched the blunt from me.

"But, dang, Red! We need to be able to go somewhere without fighting."

Goldie laughed. "That just ain't possible with a fucking friend like Red."

"Fuck bitches! Bottom line!"

Goldie said, "You gonna live to regret them words one day, girlie."

"Whatever. But we put them in their place."

"Is that what you call it? The bitch beat your ass ho."
Cha burst out laughing.

"Well, that's why I got friends. My girls always gonna bail me out no matter what."

Chapter 7

Cha

Now of course, in the beginning, setting up dudes for money all started off as fun. We had a boring life at first. Goldie lived from man to man, watching music videos, Red smoked weed all day and shot craps with the fellas, and I was raising my son Omari.

While I got by on my county check and my low-income rent, Goldie got by on a social security check. The heiffa had told them she was suffering from schizophrenia and was getting a thousand bucks every month. Plus, she also lived in the same building as me. Her mental illness allowed her access to low-income housing.

And how did Red get in? She slept with the manager. She had no additional income, except what she got from hustling. That girl done did everything under the sun to make ends meet, some I didn't even want to know about.

But some innocent thing led us up to doing some of the things we did.

Goldie was dating a dude, and one day she found out he had a woman and three kids. She pulled the old "I'm-pregnant" role, so she could get a quick three hundred bucks. Of course, dude gave it, to get rid of any evidence that he had an affair.

Then Red upped the ante a little. When Goldie was preparing to break up with him, she said, "Don't dump him until we stick his ass for some real dough."

So one day while he was over, his head all up in Goldie's twat, Red went snapping away on her disposable camera. He didn't see her. She was in the closet. And he didn't hear her 'cause they was bumping Too Short. She got him with Goldie doing him cowgirl-style and her foot in his mouth.

After a shopping spree at the Beverly Center, Goldie sat down for lunch with him at The Cheesecake Factory.

Red strolled by, slipped the pics onto the table, smacked 'ole boy on the side of his head and quickly walked away.

"What in the fuck!" Gregory said, surprised. His eyes widened once he scanned the photos, while Goldie quietly munched on her huge slice of snicker cheesecake.

He buried his head in his palms. "What do you want, Goldie?"

She twirled some of the caramel off her snicker cheesecake with her finger and licked it. "Five G." She met his gaze calmly.

"Why are you doing this?"

"'Cause you shouldn't have lied to me, muthafucka." She slid another piece of cheesecake into her mouth, chewed, and swallowed. "Now what you should be asking me is, do I have duplicates of these photos? And, yes, I do. Underneath the one of you licking my pussy is the receipt. I made three sets of copies. See." She giggled.

Gregory didn't even bother looking at the receipt. He just pulled out a check and wrote the requested amount. "After this we are done."

Goldie stood with her bags. "Yeah, whatever. Fuck you! I can do better. Now take me home before I change my mind and go visit wifey."

Gregory took a deep breath and paid the two-hundred-dollar tab Goldie ran him out of on the table. Then he followed her out. What 'ol boy didn't know was that Red had mailed off the pictures to his wife anyway.

Anyhow, when we met back up with Goldie, she tossed Red five hundred for snapping the shots and two hundred at me, really just 'cause I was her girl. One thing about Goldie, she was a very giving person.

Now, Red, if you needed someone's wig pushed back, she was good at getting that done. And she always had ideas of what else we could do.

I sat on a bench at the playground in the 'litos while Omari went down the slide. I had just picked him up from the little preschool also located in the 'litos.

I chuckled when Goldie pulled up bumping Keyshia Coles "Let It Go." The dude she was messing with now must have done something to piss her off.

"Auntie Goldie!" Omari cried.

She hopped out of the car and was talking loud on her cell phone, her bronze-colored weave flying all around her head on this windy day. "Muthafucka, you don't own me! So you paid a couple of my bills. That don't mean shit!"

I sighed and wondered if I'd have it together this time for Christmas. I always seemed to pull it off, but this time I didn't know.

"You simple-ass nigga! You got shit twisted!" Frowning, she slammed the phone closed as she came to the sidewalk. She glanced up at me and Omari, who waved at her.

She shook her head and waved back.

"Hey, girl," I said as she walked toward me carrying a tan paper box in her hands and a plastic bag. It was our lunch from Ramonas, a Mexican joint in Gardena. And yeah, we lived in Long Beach but Ramonas burritos were so good you'd drive even further to eat one. It was something about the chunks of tender beef soaked in spicy red and green chili that always had me drooling.

She let out a breathless, "Hey, Cha. Hey, boyfriend!" She plopped down next to me, sat the box on her lap and handed the bag to me. In it were two canned sodas and a chocolate milk for Omari.

"Hi," he chirped, running over and plopping down next to us.

"What's up with you? Who you going off on?"

Goldie opened the box and handed me two burritos before grabbing one for herself. "That fool, J, think 'cause he paying my cell phone bill, he can harass me."

I chuckled and sat Omari's burrito in his lap. "Take your time and eat it Omari."

Just then we heard someone speeding up the street, blasting Lil Wayne. It was Red in her red chromed-out Monte Carlo. She came so fast, skid marks came with her ass. She squeezed into a spot and was out in a flash and rushing toward us when something caught her eye. It was some ho walking in the opposite direction, across the street.

I pulled my little AM/FM walkman out of my purse and slid it over to Omari. I got it at the dollar store specifically for moments like these. I shoved them in his ears.

"Can he hear me?" Goldie asked after biting into her burrito.

I shook my head and dug into mine.

"Good. What is that crazy bitch doing?"

Red was up in this girl's face. Red shoved her and was pointing her finger all in her face.

Next thing we know, the girl pulled something out of her purse and handed it to Red. Then Red shoved her again and ran across the street toward us, while the chick scurried away.

"What's up, hoes?"

I pierced her with a look and nodded.

Goldie asked her, "And what the hell was that?"

She sat down next to both of us and pulled the money out. "I just taxed that dumb bitch."

"Taxed her?" I asked.

"Yeah, that bitch know this is Damu's jurisdiction. Other pimps even know hoes can make money over here, and she over here free-agenting. So I taxed her ass."

Goldie laughed. "You so stupid. Tell me something, Red. Is there ever a limit to what your ass won't do?"

She paused and licked her thin lips. "I don't know yet. I doubt it though. But both y'all bitches need to shut the fuck up 'cause dinner is on me." She then sat down next to Goldie and snatched the box with the burritos in it. "Bitch you better have a green chili burrito in here."

"Its in there Red," Goldie told her.

"Goldie, I can't believe your greedy ass drove all the way to Gardena for a fucking burrito."

"'Cause they got the best burritos and you know it Red," I told her.

She shrugged, pushed down the wrapper and took a man-sized bite out of hers.

I glanced at Omari who was taking another bite out of his. He liked the green chili too.

"So what's the plan, ladies? And I don't mean a day

plan to get a couple of dollars." Goldie looked at me and Red intensely. "I'm talking about a life plan."

I held in my laugh. Not wanting to crack up, I didn't bother looking at Red. Goldie often did this speech at the beginning of each month.

"'Cause this week a sista is strapped for ideas other than usual. Doing a private party is all I know about for now. And, to be honest, I'm sick of that. I'm sick of living in the projects, and I'm sick of acting psycho to get my crazy check."

"*Wawa*, bitch. Stop whining" Red said.

About once a month we did private parties, dancing for dudes. Usually in two hours we could make two hundred easy. Blue, Red's friend, always bodyguarded, so it never got out of control. It was just hard to get a lot of dudes in one place at the same time consistently.

I detested doing it. I never took off all of my clothes, which was probably why I always ended up getting cursed out and called everything but a child of God. And they always thought I was stuck-up. I couldn't take that verbal abuse more than once a month.

"Fuck a private party," Red said. "I was thinking that we do something different. I got something better to do where we can get a couple Gs a piece."

Goldie and I both leaned forward, our interest piped.

"Let's do a couple of set-ups like these niggas do."

I narrowed my eyes.

Goldie asked, "How?"

"This is what we'll do. We do a little investigation, profiling on niggas, what they go to, where they kick it. We find they ass, we go there being on point, cop his high-rollin' ass. We'll date him, build a little fictitious relationship with him, or if not, find a way to convince him to take us to his crib. Find out where he keeps his money. Y'all will be tailed. For extra precaution, we bring a nigga with a burner."

"Well, what if we can't find the money?" Goldie asked. "What if he keeps it in the bank, dumb ass?"

"Don't start the twenty-one questions. You know damn well drug dealers do not fuck with no banks, and they almost always use a safe."

"Naw, I don't wanna be bothered with no gun," I said, feeling funny about doing the whole thing anyway. But truthfully, I always felt funny about all the schemes Red and sometimes Goldie came up with, but some way I always let them convince me to do them. One reason was that I always needed the extra money and if something was okay for Goldie to do, it was okay for me.

"We won't. A nigga off the block will have the gun. We can get Blue."

Goldie wanted to know, "But what if it gets back to the dude who we are?"

"It won't. 'Cause we won't fuck with local niggas." Red puffed. "We'll network in Chino, Pomona, *parts* of LA, maybe. And when we wanna have business and pleasure, we'll shoot up to Oakland. Hell, maybe even Vegas, baby!"

Goldie and I laughed.

"You dumb ass," Goldie said.

I shook my head.

"So suppose we agree to do this shit, how much you talking about? 'Cause I'm not risking my life on no nickel-and-dime bullshit," Goldie told her.

Red snapped her head in a circle and curled her tongue. "Didn't you hear me, fool? I said *high rollers?*"

"And just how are we gonna change our appearance?" I asked.

"A weave or one of those half-wigs at the beauty salon. They don't look fake like the ones hoes wear. Different makeup. But, really, we don't need nothing much 'cause they won't know us out there, but we can change our look for extra precautions."

I wasn't with it but one look at Goldie told me that she was. So I went along with it.

"We got four parts to play—The enticer, the muscle, and two backups."

"Whose gonna be the enticer?" I asked.

"Me!" Red fired.

"No!" Goldie interjected. "Cha. You know she's the prettiest."

I shrugged 'cause I didn't know what she saw in me. All I saw was the stretch marks, and no diploma or college degree.

Red smiled mischievously. "All right, ladies, let's do this shit."

Chapter 8

Cha

All this hair on my head was making me sweat to no end. No end. And the drive to this dude we was hitting up in Pomona was a ways. I was staring out the open back window, the wind blowing through the Shirley Temple half-weave, which blended in with my real hair like them Shirley Temple's was my own.

I jumped when Blue pulled the safety back on his gun.

Red slapped him upside his face. "Fool, put that safety back on!" She puffed on her Black & Milds like it was a nipple pouring out milk.

Goldie was swooping on the I-5 like she was a professional racer and bumping Jill Scott of all people at a time like this, like we were going to listen to some jazz, instead of setting somebody up.

"Yo', fuck this love bullshit!" Red slid the CD out the radio. "Put some back-that-ass-up music on."

"Bitch!" Goldie kept her eyes on the road though.

Next thing I knew, we was bumping 50 Cent's "I Get Money."

We made it to the club and parked in the cut.

Goldie looked at me and winked.

Red asked, "You ready for this, girl?"

I took a deep breath and nodded.

"It really ain't no different than gassing niggas up like we done in the past," Red explained. "But now the stakes are a lot higher 'cause we going after high rollers is all."

I stepped out of the car and proceeded to walk to the club.

Once I entered, I brushed off niggas moaning and trying to get my attention, and females mean-mugging. I ignored them clowns and chickens and went on to the bar. I stood for a moment and glanced around.

"Hey, thickness."

I spun around and did a quick inspection. Dude had it all—the Rolex, the clothes so I knew he wasn't my target. He was too damn flashy. The dude Red told me about, you wouldn't think he was more than the manager at Foot Locker. He wasn't loud by any means. And he wasn't flashy at all.

I pulled myself from the loud nigga's arms and gave his chest a small shove, to get him completely off of me. Then I sat up at the bar.

Once I got the bartender's attention, I ordered a shot of Patrón. Threw it right back, took a deep breath, keeping my eyes off the vultures. Looked around again. Tried not to make it too obvious I was looking for anyone.

I glanced at the dance floor, skimmed chickens grinding on dudes. Didn't see any one who I thought would be him.

Then someone caught my eye. He was standing in the back of the club, leaning against a wall, jeans on, a black hoodie, drink in one hand, an unlit blunt in the other. His eyes were on me too. He eased off the wall.

I got the bartender's attention again and asked for another drink, so dude wouldn't think I was watching him.

As he came over, my heart sped up. But he didn't glance my way. Instead, he motioned for the bartender. In a low, husky voice, he ordered a Crown Royal on ice. That's when he hit me with a glance.

He had some dark, hooded eyes. He threw a twenty on the table and walked away.

I threw back my second shot. From the corner of my eye, I watched him sip on his. *Did Red really case this nigga for two weeks like she said she did? What if he's broke and don't have nothing? Well, I'm here now. It's a little too late to turn back.*

I rose from the bar stool and made my way through the crowd. I felt someone grab one of my butt cheeks. I spun around and gave him an evil glare. The clown chuckled and winked at me. I cut my eyes at him and continued where I was going, facing him, my back to the crowd.

The Lil Wayne's "Lilipop" was playing.

When I made it to him, I didn't know what to say. "It's popping in here. Why you wanna be off in the shadows?" I bit my bottom lip, one of my hipbones tilted to one side.

No response. He just stared at me, his expression unreadable.

Then, out of nowhere, the cold steel from his gat was pushing up against my nose.

"Who the fuck are you?"

My heart speeded up big time!

He repeated. "Who the fuck are you?" He waited for me to answer.

He asked so calmly, I almost didn't answer. "Jade. Now can you get the gun out my face?"

"Jade," he mused, ignoring my request. "Who sent you over here?"

"Nobody. Well, the Patrón gave me a little nerve that I could step to you."

"Yeah?" His steely eyes locked on to mine.

"Yeah. Now can you move the gun please?"

He studied me for few more moments. Let his eyes slip past my eyes to the rest of me—my B-cup breasts, small waist, swell of my hips. He nodded as if I had his approval, which I needed to just *be*.

He eased the gun out of my face and slipped it back into the waistband of his pants.

By that time I was backing away and searching for an escape.

I found it in the ladies' room, but before I got fully away from him, I mumbled, "I just thought you were cute and not trying to feel me up like them other fools. My bad, though. Didn't mean no harm." I rushed in quickly.

Luckily, it was one person shy of being empty. She was putting lip-gloss on. I brushed past her as she was on her way out and went into a stall and sat down for a minute to catch my breath.

I almost didn't see the crisp, white Air Force Ones facing my stall.

He knocked on my door. "Aye."

I stood quickly and opened the door, my heart pounding.

"Hey. Didn't mean to scare you off." He looked regretful. "There's this thing about me. I don't trust anybody."

I nodded. "Understandable."

"And I don't dance neither."

I chuckled.

"Give me your number."

I mouthed the digits to him from the burn-out phone Red had got strictly for these purposes.

"So what you about to go do?" he asked.

"I don't know."

"You going home?"

"Home?" I laughed. "You offering to take me home with you?"

"Naw. You can't come to my crib. I don't get down like that. Just met you."

I felt so stupid. I hope he didn't figure out my drag.

"Why don't you go on home. I'll give you a call tomorrow."

"And I should cut my night short because . . ."

"You got a real nigga on you now. These low-budget clowns can't compete with me, that's why. So go on."

"Wait. I don't even know your name."

"They call me *Dude*." He then took out a wad of money and, without blinking, slid out five hundred-dollar bills and tucked them in my hand.

I nodded and stepped closer to him for a hug. I stretched it, trying to kiss him.

He tilted back and shook his head. "Naw."

Embarrassed again, I took a step back, and so did he. I gave him a wave and walked away.

On my way out of the club, some stupid dude grabbed me, talking some dumb rap. "Hey, thickness."

When he said that, I realized it was the same dude inside that had pushed up on me. "Please let me go." I shoved at his chest, but this time, unlike earlier, he put up a fight.

"Come on, baby. I just want one dance, that's all."

"Yeah, go on and get the fuck off of her."

I turned and saw Dude standing half a foot away from me and the guy holding me. Then in a flash, he was all up in the face of the guy holding me.

The guy holding me said, "Man, who the fuck is you, running up on me?"

"The one who will shoot first and ask questions last," Dude said dryly, his arms crossed.

"Oh, nigga, you threatening me?"

"Naw, nigga, I ain't threatening you."

The one holding on to me started digging in his pockets. I assumed it was for a gun.

Dude was unfazed. "You too drunk to know just who the fuck I am, but I'm gonna tell you this. You pull that shit out, you betta bust, 'cause I'm for sure gonna bust mine if you make me waste the time getting it out."

He froze, thinking about what Dude said.

Another dude came out and said, "My bad, big homie. Don't pay him no mind. He just high." He pushed his friend, and they both rushed away.

Dude nodded at me, and I turned around nervously and walked away.

I went home shaken the fuck up. There was something about this man that had me nervous. Maybe it was the fact that he seemed like he was a stone-cold killer. Just knowing that he now knew I existed made me nervous as heck.

The next day I demanded to know from Red when this mess would be done.

"Patience," she told me, widening her eyes. "Play the muthafucking role, Cha. Like you one of them innocent girls who don't kiss on the first date and won't fuck until twenty -twenty."

"Shit! Cha is one of those girls," Goldie said, cracking up and slapping one of her thighs.

Red laughed. She clasped her fingers together. "Then we shouldn't have any problems getting in his damn pockets."

***

When we chilled at Red's pad a few days later, I demanded to know again, "How long will this 'ish' take?" After the first meeting after the club and having him all up in my grill, and his hands all over my butt, I wanted this mess over.

Red, stretched out on her bed on a dirty comforter like she was a don, puffed on my Black & Milds. I even thought she really believed she was a don.

"I'll give it three more dates. You already got one down. On the next one, let him kiss you, on the third, eat your pussy, and on the fourth date, you'll be all up in his pad."

On the second date, I let him rub my ass and suck on my earlobe. On the third date, he took me on a shopping spree at a mall he said he frequented in Pomona.

He slid ten hundred-dollar bills in my hand and said, "I got phone calls to make. I ain't got time to walk around with you, although I wouldn't mind following you around to keep these simple niggas off you. But something tells me you ain't no fool like I ain't no fool. I know a dime piece when I see it, smell it, and I'm sure you know a connected nigga when you see him."

I nodded and smiled, licking my lips. He smacked me on my ass as I headed out of his shiny black Escalade. I heard him say, "Don't forget to buy some lingerie."

And I shopped. Primarily, I bought some things Omari needed, clothes, three pairs of shoes and a jacket. I went to Victoria's Secret and purchased lingerie like he requested. I stuffed all of Omari's things in an big empty Macys bag. I spent a cool six hundred. Four hundred on Omari, one hundred on lingerie and one hundred on his shirt. Then I bought him a really nice dressy shirt for effect and pocketed the rest. I mean, it was quick thinking. I was hoping he didn't ask me to show him what I bought.

When I made it back to the car, he was still on the phone. He glanced my way and muttered real quick, "Let me hit you back."

I put my bags in the back, except for the bag with his gift.

He eyed me as I slid into the front seat. He bit his bottom lip. "You enjoyed yourself?"

I nodded. "Yes, thank you."

"You know it can be like this all the time. That kind of money ain't shit to me. I make that in a matter of minutes."

"I appreciate your generosity, and I got you something just out of appreciation." I slid the bag his way.

He opened it, glanced inside, and busted a quick smile. "Thanks, baby."

I leaned over and kissed him.

He gripped my waist in one hand, yanking me off the seat so he could grip one of my butt cheeks in the other. "How did I get so lucky to find a woman sweet like you out here?"

I lowered my lids and smiled. "Maybe we both got lucky."

He didn't say anything else, just started his truck, and rolled down the highway.

All the while during the ride I was wondering, *Am I in yet?*

Chapter 9

Cha

I was in. And I was scared as hell. Guess there was something about my little generosity, and the way I swung my rump in my dress he had surprised me with on the previous date, along with a matching pink thong and bra that made him feel so comfortable with me.

He pulled into a long driveway, turned off the ignition and turned to me.

"Now I don't usually do this. I trust no one." His eyes were serious, almost steely. "But you, Jade, you getting under my skin, making a businessman like myself wanna break some rules for you."

I offered a smile. "You got me breaking a couple rules too, Dude."

"Oh, yeah?"

We both exited the car and made it up the steps to his house. Red said the fourth date. I was making progress, 'cause this was the third.

Once I was inside, it sure was hard to case his place when he was right on me, rubbing his hands across my butt, and every step I took, he took, like we were waltzing. *Dang! Be easy, dude. Could I live? Could I breathe?*

The main thing I needed to know was where he kept

his dough. Inside his mattress? In a safe? Where? And how the hell was I going to find out? It wasn't like he was going to volunteer the information to me anyway.

As I passed his lavish living room with huge plasma flat-screens on his walls, TVs, plush couches, and black marble-cased floors, I saw a fish tank embedded in a wall. It looked like a baby shark was in the tank.

He yanked me to face him. "Give me a kiss, baby."

I did and attempted to keep up with his heavy tongue action.

He grabbed my hips and lifted me so that my thighs were curved around his waist, and carried me into his bedroom. He tossed me backward on the bed, walked over to his dresser, and sat his wallet and gun on it. The bed was so high my feet dangled from it.

Before I could even catch my breath, he was on top of me, kissing me, rubbing my breasts. He then eased his way down to my pussy, all the while eyeing me. "Is your pussy as sweet as your mouth, Jade?"

I was nervous and wanted to run out of his crib, but I smiled in a sexy way. "Guess you gonna have to see. Huh, daddy?"

He wasn't my baby, Onyx, but a brother knew what he was doing down there. Still, I couldn't bring myself to enjoy it.

After ten minutes of him kissing and sucking, and rubbing his fingers where he tasted me, I knew I would have to find a way to stop this. But I didn't have to. The doorbell rang.

He kept on licking. I guess he was hoping that, if he ignored the person who continued to ring it, they would go away. They didn't.

He hopped up and without looking at me said, "Sit tight. I'll be right back."

Once he slipped from the room, I quietly rose from the bed and went to the bedroom door.

I peeked out just as he was opening the front living room door and saw another dude behind it.

"You early. I was doing something."

It was that same menacing tone I had got acquainted with when we first met, when he got the guy from the club off of me and, really, the same tone he had used with me. But after that day, this was the first time I had heard him use that tone again.

I grimaced as he wiped his face with his hand, trying to get my juices off him.

"Well, I had to get the supply now. We out, and we need to cook some more before five or you going to lose out on a lot of dough, Dude."

Dude just stared at the guy. It appeared he was making him nervous.

The guy looked up to the sky, behind him, then at his shoes, before asking, "Can I come in?"

"No. Wait on the steps."

I snuck back in bed when I heard Dude's footsteps. I kept my eyes down like I was looking at my fingernails, but I was looking at what he was doing and his positioning.

I watched in amazement as he flipped open the flat-screen TV. There behind the flat-screen, he shifted over to the right.

Had to be. Yeah, it was his safe.

He pulled four white bags out and quickly shut the safe, but I still saw all the stacked bills, all of his money.

"I'll be back," he said.

"Okay. Hurry, baby."

Once he exited the room, I jumped to my feet with my purse and rushed into his bathroom. My phone was on vibrate. I peeled it out of my purse. I didn't have time to read all the text messages I had that were probably from Red and Goldie, so I scrolled down until I saw Red's number. I texted her, **I'm here. Found the safe. 1232 E Mission Blvd off white house.** I pressed send, took a deep breath, and closed my phone.

A fist struck the bathroom door. My heartbeat speeded up, and I almost pissed in my pants. I forgot to lock the door.

"What you doing?" he demanded in a suspicious tone.

I thought of something quick. "I needed to get myself ready. I'll be out in a minute."

"Get ready? Shit! How you gonna get more ready than you were when I was eating your pussy?"

"I use a diaphragm."

Silence. Made my heart beat faster. It was one of those situations where you don't know whether to move or freeze. If I stayed frozen, he could open the door and see the phone in my hand. If I move, the sound could seem suspicious and send him in the bathroom.

Finally, he said, "Oh."

I took a deep breath. *Good thinking.* When I felt the phone vibrate, I coughed, to offset the sound. He didn't say anything. Maybe he didn't hear it.

"Hurry out, baby."

I heard his footsteps as he walked away from the door. I took a deep breath, stuffed the phone in my purse, hoping they would get their butts here soon.

I sighed and stripped out of my pants, my fingers shaking, heart pounding as I did this. Would I ever get used to this? Probably not. But they were leaning on me getting this right, so I had to.

I stepped out clad in my thong and bra, so he'd really believe I was getting myself ready. *Please get here in time.*

He was stretched out in the bed. His head shot up when the bathroom door opened.

I thought quickly. While I stood there and he watched me from the bed, biting his bottom lip, I asked him, "Would you like for me to dance for you, baby? I know it's not much to make up for how good you been to me, but it's something."

He licked his lips. "Yeah." He turned over on his stomach and reached for his remote.

As I wound my hips in a circular motion to the sounds of T-Pain wafting through the room, he was transfixed.

"Turn around."

I did, and gave him a full view of my ass which was barely concealed by my lacy pink thong. I rubbed my mounds of flesh in my hand, hoping they would hurry up and get here. I jiggled my butt cheeks. I grasped my breast in the palms of my hands and pushed them together.

He gave that groan in his throat again. He grabbed his dick, massaged it, grunted deep in his throat, and continued to watch me. He pulled a blunt from his pocket and lit it. He puffed and watched, his eyes getting hooded by the second.

I slid my tongue from my lips and traced the nipple of my left breast.

He took a puff and blew out, slowly. Then he tilted his head back.

I traced my other nipple with my tongue. I slid my hands down my body past my breast to my belly button, down over my thong underwear.

He dropped the blunt in an ashtray on the nightstand and started rubbing his dick with both hands.

I displayed my fingers on my pussy, pushing my pelvis upward. My heart was pounding 'cause I knew any moment he would say, "Come here, baby." And he did.

I kept my face cool. Well, God, I hoped I did. I walked over to him slowly, hoping to distract him by the way I swayed. I crawled onto the bed and edged my way toward him slowly, one knee at a time.

"You ready for this, daddy?" I asked.

"Yeah, I'm ready." He looked down at his erection, threatening to bust out from his pants and split his legs open for me to sit between them.

Guess he wanted head. With shaking hands, I went for his belt to unbuckle his pants.

That's when Blue kicked open the door and busted through.

Dude pushed me away. I guess he was gonna go for his strap, but he had put it on the dresser, not the nightstand right across from us, along with his wallet, right when we first walked in his bedroom.

I screamed and fell to the floor.

"Don't move, muthafucka, or I'm gonna blow you and this bitch away!"

I peeked up from the floor and saw the angry look on Dude's face. He didn't move from his spot on the bed.

"Where?" Blue pointed the gun at Dude, angled it in his face.

Dude ignored him, so Blue started throwing shit around, I guess, trying to play it off so it didn't look like a set-up of sorts.

After trashing his stereo and knocking over furniture, he went to the flat-screen. "Oh, you think you smart."

"Fuck you," Dude said, calmly.

"Naw, nigga, fuck you! 'Cause you getting fucked in the ass with no K-Y Jelly!"

I sniffled like I was really scared.

"Shut up, bitch!" Blue yelled.

All I saw was green, and bags of white being stuffed in Blue's bag, along with Dude's gun, wallet, and some jewelry he had on his dresser.

Dude's eyes burned into Blue.

"That yo' woman, Dude?"

"No, the bitch ain't my woman."

That made my heart beat faster. I wished we could be done with this shit.

"Well, you don't mind if I take her ass with me, do you?"

"Yeah, take her and leave my money."

"Can't do that, but I will for sure take her fine ass off your hands."

I started sobbing harder, and Dude's face softened toward me.

"Get what you getting, and get the fuck out."

Blue, backing out of the room, continued to aim his gun at us.

After we heard Blue's car tires squeak, Dude started cursing and throwing shit around in his room. He picked up his phone and called somebody.

"Yo', get here now! I been robbed. The nigga just left!"

Ten minutes later

I kept the same solemn look on my face as I was passed to another dude.

"Take her home."

I was ushered into one car, while Dude got into another, loading his gun with bullets. Just before the car pulled off, he turned and looked directly at me. "I'm gonna find his ass."

I desperately wanted to text Red to see how far they were and warn them, but I didn't want to look suspicious, since his homie in the car kept his eyes on me the whole ride.

"Where you stay at?" he asked me.

Chapter 10

Goldie

Leave it to Red to give me the most fucked up assignment. I was over at some spot in Marina Del Rey. Supposed to be some white dude. And he was throwing a party.

"This one is super easy Goldie. The only problem you have to worry about is saying no. 'Cause these mothafuckas like to party. They snort coke and walk around like zombies.

He seemed pretty much harmless. But Red said he kept washed money for serious drug dealers from Northern to Southern California.

I asked her, "Does he have dough at home?"

"Yes! Girl, yes! You gotta trust me."

So I did, but I had a gat of my own in my purse for protection. Couldn't believe Cha didn't think to have one on the first one we did. There was something about Dude that made me feel like she was gonna see him again.

When I walked in that house, I felt like I was in Satan's Den. First a dyke looking female came toward me wearing a leather black cape and said, "Welcome to our little family." Then she winked at me. When she turned around I almost gasped at the chain hanging down between her legs.

I smiled and said, "Thank you." But inside I wanted to kick Red's punk ass when I saw what the fuck she brought me into. A damn swinger's party.

"Trinity told me all about you."

Trinity was the chick that Red had hooked up with to do this little scheme. She became a part of the whole swingers crew for this whole set-up. I wondered what all she had to do to be "a part" of it. I sure as hell was not going to engage in any of this.

She turned around and caught my snarled up face. I quickly smiled as I came into the dim lit room.

"Would you like one of these?"

"One of what?"

She turned around, faced me and pulled one side of her cape away. "This."

I gasped when I saw the tip of the chain hanging from her shaved pussy.

"I'm good." You sick bitch. I wanted to yell.

She shrugged and giggled. "Suit yourself. Follow me."

As we walked further down the corridor she put her arm out and allowed me full entrance into the house. One look at them mothafuckas and I wanted to run out of the room.

To my right a black girl was lying flat on her back while a white girl was shoving a dildo in her coochie. A few inches from them a white dude dressed in all leather was humping a black dude doggie style!

The shit made me wanna throw up.

There were two ninety pound white chicks on a couch who looked like they were dying from anorexia. I swallowed the urge to vomit again while watching one lying on her back and the other had her bleach blonde head between her legs. She pulled her face up when she felt my presence. Her mouth and chin had the other girl's fluid gliding down it. She offered me a smile and beckoned me closer with a finger. The other girl continued shivering and holding her breasts in her hands.

I turned my head.

"Care to join them?"

"No."

That's when a black girl with a dozen different piercings on her face and body brushed past me buck naked and joined their little circle. She crouched above the girl who was getting her thing thing ate out and that girl went to work on her.

I narrowed my eyes as she threw her head back in pleasure. She picked up one of her sagging titties and let her pierced tongue flicker across her nipple. She had to be Trinity. She fit Red's description.

I tried to keep my face normal. Like I came to houses like this all the time when I wanted to bash these nasty bastards in the head with a crow bar. There were other people in the room. They stood around watching the show and some of the dudes jacked off and some of the chicks masturbated to it.

Then in the center of the room I saw him sitting on a chair. I couldn't really see his face, but I assumed he was Arthur.

"So now that you have seen everything, are you still interested in being a member?"

I nodded.

Her eyes locked with mine. "Great. Let me introduce you to our host. All memberships are approved by him and by him only. But I'm sure he will approve you. You're stunning."

My heart sped up and we walked toward him. He was seated in the center of the room watching everything. I had not even noticed him but he probably had been watching me. I was trying to remember what I was supposed to do after I was introduced to him. But I forgot all about the plan.

The closer we got the more scared I was. They said this place was safe but all these sickos? And in all honesty, who's to say they didn't have guns?

The dude looked like he was six feet four inches. His head was totally bald and he had some cold blue eyes. I hope he didn't see through the bullshit.

"Liam, this is . . ."

He silenced her with a hand and pierced me with a look. "Who invited you?"

I gestured toward Trinity.

He nodded. Then he stood to his feet. "Come with me."

As I walked behind him, my hand rested over the imprint of the gun in my purse 'cause if he tried to rape me he was gonna be one dead white boy.

He guided me with one hand, killing off any opportunity to slip out my phone and text them. I had no idea where his safe was and didn't know how I was going to find out. Before we even got the chance to slip up the stairs Blue and a dressed-like-a-dude busted in the house and came rushing in the den.

I spun around and so did Liam.

But once Red and Blue saw what they saw, they hesitated. I pulled myself from Liam's grasp and rushed toward the door.

"Y'all mothafuckas get the fuck down!" Blue shouted.

"You didn't text us," Blue said looking around.

"Kiss my ass!" I fired back. Then as I made it to the door I said, "Y'all some sick mothafuckas!" I pointed around to all of them while saying, "You. You. You and you! I'm praying y'all stop this sick shit!" Then I slipped out of the door.

Chapter 11

Goldie

I must say that these little licks had us sitting pretty on dough. Blue, for his troubles, either kept the dope we found, or we would toss him a few hundred. But we always got the bulk of it and always came out decent.

But, poor Cha, she'd been through some shit with the last lick. For starters, the dude, I think she kind of liked, and she had left her purse there. That had her real nervous. It would've had my ass scared too 'cause Dude looked like a straight killer. Which Red told me he was. That was kind of scandalous of her ass. She should have warned Cha ahead of time about what she was getting involved in. But that's Red for ya. She didn't mean no harm; she was just reckless as hell, is all.

I didn't blame Cha for wanting to back out. She told us both, "I don't care what y'all bitches say. The only way I'm doing another lick is if, and only if, one or both of y'all accompany me."

We knew she wasn't playing 'cause Cha rarely cursed. And when she was really mad or shocked, she'd say, "W-T-F!"

Cha had put herself on the line for all of us with Dude. And she had more to lose, which was little Omari.

So tonight it was the three musketeers on a mission, me, Red, and Cha. This dude was Roco. Kid you not. Yep, Red sure knew how to pick them. But she wanted to put us in the line of fire. At first, the go-to girl was an issue only because Red wanted to be known as the prettiest, but when there was danger involved, she wanted no part of it. I busted her shit-colored ass on that shit.

She twisted her thin lips to the side and said, "I mean, I'm the one doing all the profiling, picking the spots. Shit! To me that should suffice."

"Well, it ain't tonight. We all gonna do this shit." I didn't give a damn if it made her ass mad.

"Okay. Damn! You and Cha complain too much."

So a week later she found us an assignment.

"We all gonna be in on this one," she told me, Cha, and Blue as we chilled over at her pad. "Ain't no need for us to scope nothing out. I did that. Ain't no need for no dates. He does everything from his car."

"Huh?" Cha asked, confused as I was.

"He do his shit from his car. He sells his drugs there, keeps up to fifteen Gs in his glove compartment. So that's where we will do our lick. Now dude is blind in one eye, and the other one is going out lazy. He in his thirties and he got some type of flesh eating shit and it's eating his face away."

Me and Cha looked at each other.

"Flesh eating? What in the hell? Red you sure know how to pick these fools!"

"Goldie shut the fuck up and listen."

I flipped her the bird.

She ignored me.

"He ain't gonna be hard to spot. He gon' be the orang-utan-looking muthafucka, wearing nice clothes. And he loves bitches. Beautiful, fly bitches!"

This sounded easy.

The meet-up place was The Penthouse, a strip club in LA, off El Segundo.

Red flat-ironed her hair and wore a red skimpy dress. Cha was turning heads, of course, in a wife-beater, black jeans, and heels. I had on a Baby Phat cat suit I got on sale at Ross. Men stared at us more than them tired-ass strippers.

And Roco? Yeah, Roco was in VIP. And, yes, the muth-afucka was ugly. So ugly, he was hard to look at without me wanting to shake my head and say, "Bless his heart," or yell out like Shug did in *The Color Purple* to Celie, "'You sho is ugly!'"

But, hell, his dollars weren't. Green never ain't. They make the person whose hand they being held in look finer than a muthafucka. But him, hell, he was still ugly.

All I could say as he held them presidents was, "He cool," but he really wasn't. He was guzzling from a Moët bottle like it was water.

As we walked to the VIP section, Red was making her titties jiggle. I was whipping my hips so hard and fast, my ass wobbled against my back, while all Cha did was look around coyly.

Roco was too fixated on the naked stripper in front of him to even notice us until I got slick and sent him over a bottle of Hennessy.

He was tossing fifty after fifty on that ho jiggling her money-making ass for him. Cha grimaced, Red looked on, probably wishing it were her.

I had the urge the snatch up the dough off the chick's sweaty ass and run out on that bitch. We heard him yell to the waitress who brought over the Hennessy courtesy of us.

"You see what I drink? Me no drink dat?" He shoved an empty Moët bottle toward her. "Me asked for chree! Chree bottles a dis not dat!"

The waitress rolled her eyes like his breath stank. She pointed her finger in our direction. "They sent it over."

He blocked the strobe light and got a good look at us. He licked his lips then. He checked all of us out. Bust into a fucked-up, ugly-ass smile.

"Ouuu, no," I said.

"Yeah, that bitch is ugly." Red shook her head.

Cha gave a sad smile, you know the type when you see an ugly baby. You wanna say, "Damn!" But you wanna be nice, so you offer that smile.

We all tipped our glasses to him.

Next thing we knew, he was sending us bottle after bottle. And we was getting tipsy and damn near forgot what we came for.

I stood up and started wiggling, and Red started slapping me on my ass. To our right, Cha was bending over and making her cheeks do a dance on their own couldn't no one imitate. That's when I looked in the corner of my eye to see if we had managed to capture his attention.

He was glancing at us, past the stripper's ass, so I thought quick and lay across the table on my back and let Red pour some drink on my exposed belly button and lick it off. Let him think we were some dyke bitches. What man didn't love that? A fine-ass dyke bitch? Shit!

But I don't care what Red said. She was enjoying the shit a bit too much. I almost punched her ass when she kissed me dead on my lips, but I played it off. Pulled my lips back and massaged her big ass.

Then he was making his way over to our table. We had him.

I winked at him and said loudly, "Hey, papa. Glad you gunning for a real woman, a real pussy, and some real fun."

"He didn't speak but quickly turned me around and started grinding all up against me.

When Red got in on the action, bending over beside him, he started smacking her on the ass.

"Whew! Shit, daddy! Wish you was hitting me with yo' dick!" Red giggled.

"You want dis dick?" he asked in his thick accent.

Cha got in on the action by stepping to him and pouring more drink down that mongoloid throat of his.

Once we tired him out, I sat him down in the chair. Cha sat on his lap, and Red, across from him. He was able to stick his fingers in her pussy from underneath the table.

I stood behind him and massaged his neck. I bent over and slipped the tip of my tongue in his ear. "You wanna take this somewhere private, Mr. Reggae?"

"Come!"

We followed behind him as he exited the club. Blue was supposed to meet us in the parking lot, pull out his gun and steal dude's keys, drive off, strip the dough and we find a way for him to scoop us up once we managed to slip away from ugly.

As we walked to his car, we didn't see Blue. I tossed a glance back to Red.

She discreetly tried to text him. She raised her brows as if to say, "Nothing."

"Me got chocolate," he said, gesturing to Cha. He gestured to me—"Milk chocolate"—and then to Red. "White chocolate."

We all smiled.

Red said, "Yeah, daddy, you do, and I want you to get a taste of my chocolate first."

"Me wanna fuck that pumm pumm ," he said then groaned, slapping Red on her ass." His pace got quicker.

Shit! I thought as we followed him. Where in the fuck was Blue's ass?

"Let's see . . . I park in the aisle chree." He turned a corner, bent over, and bit Cha on her ass.

She screeched.

He laughed out loud. "Smoke?" he asked us.

"I do," Red said.

"Okay, man. We can light one up some of that good shit." He pressed a button, and his Benz lighted up next to a white Volvo.

I tossed another look at Red. She ignored it. What the fuck was going on?

Both me and Cha were prepared to hop in the back, leaving Red no choice but to sit up front. Cha slipped in and I followed after her. Before I could even sit down comfortably, I was shoved and the car door was slammed.

I screamed as Blue shoved his gun in the window of the car.

Cha screamed next, followed by Red, but her dumbass scream sounded fake.

"Give it up, you fucking foreigner."

Roco froze.

"You heard what I said, ugly."

"Batty Boy!"

That's when we heard it. *Bam!*

I looked at Blue horrified, but he looked at me and shrugged. It took me a few seconds to realize that the shot didn't come from Blue's gun, but from Roco's.

We all ducked and screamed.

Blue ducked down and ran to the back of the car.

"You try to rob me!" Roco fired another shot without even turning his head to look where the fuck he was shooting at. He pointed the gun in the direction of the back seat and fired.

I stayed ducked down, my heart thudding. From the corner of my eye I saw Cha was the first to be brave enough to even move. Like grease lightning, she opened the car door on her side. I heard a thud and after, her heels hitting the concrete.

It didn't stop Roco from firing. "Me kill you too bitch."

He aimed his gun in the direction of Cha.

That's when Red and I got the balls to flee.

Blue was ducked behind the car and started firing back at Roco.

Red and I both took off running and screaming.

The shots continued ringing out behind us.

Where was Cha? I glanced behind me as I kept running

Then I heard the engine of Roco's Benz and saw it make a u-turn and Buju Banton was blasting. I glanced back and saw his ugly-ass face in the window.

"Shit!" I screamed terrified.

"Bumbaclat ! Bitches trying to rob me!" I ran quicker as I saw the car speeding down one aisle while we were running down another. Thank God he was drunk and couldn't shoot worth a damn. The bullets went every which way, hitting car windows, cars and even setting off alarms. People in the parking lot had to choose to either join us in running or drop to the ground.

But the nigga kept coming toward us yelling out shit I didn't understand.

"Ras clot !"

I screamed at the top of my lungs as the car came speeding toward me and Red. I already claimed one of the bullets.

Before I got the chance to even look back at his ugly ass face, the car came to a screeching crash into another parked car. Reckless ass.

***

Me and Red stayed in the cut as if we were some innocent bystanders and not the bitches that tried to set Roco up. Once the ambulance rushed his ass away and the police were done doing their investigating, Red and I came out of the crowd of people. I was starting to worry again, because we still had not seen Cha.

"Where do you think she is? I asked Red.

She shrugged. "You think she went back in the club?"

"I fucking hope so, Red." But the more seconds went by the more I started to worry until I was running up and down the parking lot rows sniffling and yelling out, "Cha! Cha!"

I hoped one of those bullets had not claimed my friend. With each car I passed I was dreading seeing my friend lying in a pool of her own blood. It got to the point that my shoulders were shaking and I starting bawling like a baby. I balled up both my fist and hit them on my thighs. I yelled out, "Ch-Chandria! Cha!" At the top of my lungs.

That's when I heard someone whisper, "Goldie. I'm over here."

My head shot up. I still didn't see her.

I spun around. "Cha?" I demanded.

"Yes."

My eyes narrowed. "Where are you?"

"I know this bitch is not underneath the car!" Red shouted. She must have just managed to catch up with me.

I crawled on my knees to where the voice was, two cars past where we were, and sure enough, that's where she was. Underneath a white Magnum.

She slid from under the car saying, "Ain't nobody taking me away from Omari,"

I fell on my back and busted up laughing. Red stood staring at us and mumbling, "Muthafucking Blue."

Finally when Blue pulled up, we dove in, and he skidded the fuck off!

Chapter 12

Red

Shit. I realized after that fiasco, I had to find other ways to make money because set-ups were just plain-out too risky.

I slapped Blue four times. "You stupid muthafucka! You didn't do shit like we planned!"

"Well, shit, I did what the fuck I knew!" He screamed at the top of his lungs, slapping his hands together. "Y'all bitches should have checked to see if the gun was on him when y'all was grinding y'all stank pussies on 'em."

That got us all riled up.

We all started slapping him upside his head, yelling out, "Who you calling bitches?"

He screamed, "Y'all bitches, get the fuck out my ride!" He pulled over.

We ignored his punk ass, so he ended up getting back in traffic.

I gave his head another slap. "You stupid muthafucka!"

But I had other methods of making money. Some might call them unconventional, but I call y'all muthafuckas, 'cause y'all wasn't paying my rent. Really, my side gig that was starting to increase was my networking for Damu. He was a popular "folk" in Long Beach, Compton, and Los Angeles, meaning a pimp. I was finding him hoes and checking hoes out of pocket. Sometimes I felt like I was babysitting them bitches.

Case in point, today I was with Ginger. The little ho had got herself knocked up, so she was trying to get an abortion. The dummy had some abandonment issues, being that her mom sold her to Damu for four crack rocks.

Naturally, she wanted to keep the baby, but Damu wasn't having that shit, and she knew it. He had given me a quick fifty to escort her ass to the clinic, and I'd get another fifty once she dropped the little bastard she was carrying through them tubes. That meant I had to stay with her ass.

We sat in the waiting room I flipped through a magazine. I wasn't even reading, but I didn't want her to start talking to me.

She turned her Bambi eyes on me and said, "I'm scared, Red."

I wanted to say, "So, ho?" but, hell, she was thirteen. "It will be okay. I get this shit done all the time." Wrong. I even gave her a tight smile before going back to the magazine.

"But it's a sin."

So is ho'ing, you dumb ass. I looked the other way, to the left side of the waiting room toward some bitches staring me down. Already irritated by this young bitch, I banged on them. "Damn! I wish bitches would stop fucking staring!"

Ginger giggled and clasped a hand over her mouth. "Ouu! You crazy, Red. I'm irritated by those bitches too. You remind me of myself."

I gave her a half-smile, thinking all the while, *Naw, bitch, you could never be like me.*

"So, Red, what's your real name?"

"Reagen," I said dryly.

"Reagen? Why yo' mama name you that?"

I almost snapped. "I don't know." The last thing I wanted to discuss was her ass. I hoped that bitch had rot to worms by now.

"Oh."

I breathed a sigh of relief when they finally called her dumb ass.

Thirty minutes later she emerged looking like someone fucked her in the ass.

That was quick, I thought. I stood up and offered a tight smile.

As we exited the place and were on the way to my car parked on the street, some white lady approached us and handed me a brochure. I looked at her confused.

She smiled and said, "Here's some literature, dear."

"For what?"

"Well, when a woman has an abortion, she tends to become severely depressed and often wants to kill herself."

I flung the brochures back at her, so they slapped her in the face. "Bitch, I ain't had no abortion! I'm more likely to kill your ass before I'd ever kill myself!" I slapped the brochures she had in her other hand to the ground.

Her whole face dropped. She nodded. "God bless you."

I twisted my lips to one side. "Yeah, you too, *biatch.*"

Ginger laughed again and followed behind me. "You are so crazy!"

I ignored her and walked to my car located on the street to the right of the clinic. I unlocked my car and made her ass wait until I was in my car comfortably before I leaned over and unlocked the passenger side for her.

I started the car, and blasted Lil Wayne before heading down the road to drop her simple ass off.

When we approached a light, she asked me, "You ever been to Cold Stone?"

I nodded my head to my music, wishing she would shut the fuck up.

"Well, have you?"

"What the fuck is Cold Stone?"

"It's an ice cream parlor. My mom took me once." Her face got sad suddenly. "Your mom ever took you?"

"Why the fuck you asking me? You want some fucking ice cream?"

"Well, since you never been."

"Where is it?"

"You just passed it."

I sped up, slid between the two broken yellow lines, and busted a U-turn. "You paying for it."

"Okay!" she said cheerfully.

I hopped out of my car and followed her into the place. That shit smelled so good, I was glad I listened to her and went up in there. But once I inspected it, the ice cream looked fucking weird, like slabs of damn meat.

"We should have went to Baskin-Robbins."

She stopped gazing at the menu. "Why?"

"'Cause! That don't look like ice cream. It looks like blocks of damn clay."

She laughed. "Girl, you pick what you want in your ice cream. You can put cookies, brownies, M&Ms, even Gummi Bears! And look"—She pointed up at the menu that I still hadn't looked at. "You can get a specialty. I always get the apple pie à la mode."

That shit sounded good.

"Man, I'm so glad I came with you. Thanks, Red."

"Yeah, no problem." My eyes passed over one that sounded cool—brownie obsession. It said brownies, caramel, pecans. I was trying to imagine how that would taste and almost didn't even hear her dumb ass.

"I mean, I'm saying, Red, I don't think I would have been able to have the guts to do what I did."

"It's just a gotdamn baby! Fuck it."

"No, not that."

The lady behind the counter said, "Ma'am, welcome to Cold Stone. What can I get for you?"

I ignored her and turned back to Ginger, my eyes narrowed. "Whatchu mean?" I wanted a reply, so I waited.

She smiled and tapped me on my shoulder. "Girl, I didn't kill my baby. Before I went into the operating room, I talked to that lady and she said I still had the op-op—"

"Option."

"Thanks, girl. Yeah, option to keep it, so I did."

I paused before asking, "You mean to tell me you still pregnant?"

"Yeah, girl. That's why I'm craving something sweet." She giggled. "Well, the baby is." She patted her tummy.

My eyes dropped to her tummy. I smiled slowly. Then I swung my foot and kicked her directly in her stomach as hard as I could.

She flew back with the force and screamed.

I cocked my foot back and swung it again, despite the cashier screaming horrified that I was kicking her. The second kick made her fly into a table and fall to the floor crying. Then I dragged the bitch to the car by her ponytail.

I needed that other fifty, and there was no way I was sending her ass back to that man preggers. Stupid little pig!

I started the ignition and took my right hand and backhanded her in her mouth, 'cause she wouldn't stop crying. "Shut the fuck up, bitch! You don't need to be nobody's mama."

When she started whimpering, I balled up my fist and shoved it in her face.

She swallowed hard, but nothing came out them vocal chords but air. She stared down at the blood seeping from her pants.

I ignored the blood and drove off. I did just what I planned on doing. I hauled her bloody ass back on the track on Long Beach Boulevard in front of the Compton Swap Meet.

Damu was out there too. He looked up surprised when I rushed up to him and threw her inches from his gator shoes.

"The bitch's baby is dead. Where my money?"

Chapter 13

Goldie

I needed some drinks 'cause this dude was coming over and I planned on getting him drunk and taking all his shit. And it was his fault I had them type of intentions.

When we'd first met, I was washing my clothes at the Laundromat, and he was passing through. When he was trying to get my digits, he talked about taking me to Lawry's, where I'd never been, The Cheesecake Factory, and Parkers' Lighthouse in Long Beach, where I'd never been.

Then, when he called me on the phone, it was a whole 'nother fucking story.

"So, Goldie, I-I really want to get to know you better."

I rolled my eyes. "Ummmm."

"Goldie, you got a DVD?"

"No!"

"What about a VCR?"

"No!"

"A T—"

"No!"

I damn well did, but fuck that nigga. Take a bitch out. I swear, niggas just didn't understand. You can get the pussy, but damn, give me one phone conversation, just one! A steak and potato, a movie, or a set of these flowers, and the pussy is yours. But these simple muthafuckas just couldn't seem to do this.

I had two bottles of Hennessy on the counter, along with my "zu-zus and wham-bams." I swiped my atm card with the swiftness.

The gay Indian dude, Sasha, who was hella cool flung his silky bob to the side. "It's declined, girl."

"What?" I was too embarrassed to say anything else.

Someone tossed a fifty on the counter. I stared back at the man in blue. What did he think I was? A fucking charity case? Fucking pig. And it wasn't just because of that. I had seen him before, about four months ago. Back then, I was dumb enough to actually date someone who lived in the Carmelitos. I listened to his sob story about getting laid off from McDonnell Douglas and that he had to come stay with his mama.

I allowed him to wine and dine me the best he could. In his case, dinner at my house. I was really feeling dude and his tongue action, and that horse dick he had. And there I was about to start making future decisions, about to yank off the condom, and have him put a baby in my stomach, with my ignorant ass, until I found out the fool was a goddamn liar and had a woman outside of the projects.

So I waited one day when he had his car parked outside his mama's house and took some glitter spray paint and prepared to fuck his car clear up. I didn't want it to be no secret it was me. I planned on writing, "Goldie did this shit!"

The whole while I'm pulling my weave back in a ponytail, taking the paint out of the bag, shaking it up and saying, "I'm gonna get this bitch."

When I noticed the cop standing right behind me, watching, I dropped the spray paint and ran like a bat out of hell. The officer didn't even bother chasing me.

I heard the Indian dude say, "Ouuu, Goldie got a policeman."

I gave him the "shut-the-fuck-up" look, and he gave me one right back, placing one hand on his hips and poking out his lip-glossed mouth.

I walked out of the store with the drink. I didn't tell his ass thank you.

I was rushing down the street when I heard someone on my heels. I turned around. It was the pig. My nostrils flared. "If you expect a muthafucking thank-you, then your ass can forget it."

He chuckled, unmoved by the fact that my right hand was on my hip and my head was moving at a 160-degree angle.

"I was trying to give you the other bag, that's all." He lifted it in the air. It had my zu-zus and wham-bams.

Now I felt like a damn fool. Not only did he pay for my shit, he was kind enough to bring my bag to me. But he still was a fucking pig.

"Thank you," I said, and I rushed off.

Chapter 14

Cha

Now the good thing about welfare wasn't the cash or the food stamps, but whenever my baby or I were sick, we could see a doctor. We also got free counseling. Omari had been getting it ever since Onyx was killed. I, however, chickened out every time I made an appointment. But lately I had been having these weird dreams. Well, I guess you could call them nightmares. I was always locked in this closet, and right before I woke up I always saw a man's face.

So my social worker referred me to this man who was supposed to be the best. I told myself when I saw him that I would be as open as I possibly could, so maybe, just maybe, he could really help me.

I wasn't expecting him to be black, but he was, and he looked like he was in his early forties. The atmosphere was cool in his nice-looking office. He offered me some coffee. Seeing that I was young, most didn't think that I touched the stuff, but I did. It calmed my nerves. It was either that or a more expensive habit to take up. Since I couldn't afford habits, I was addicted to caffeine instead.

"So tell me, Chandria, why you're here."

"I have a lot of issues, doctor. I think they are based on my past. I grew up in a group home because my mama and daddy"—I waved my hand but forced myself to go on—"They left me in a dumpster when I was a few days old. I been the property of DCFS ever since."

"How did you feel being in the group home?"

"I hated it. The food was always bad. Cereal and the same darn donut every morning. Always soup for lunch, then ham or turkey for dinner. Then they would take whatever was for dinner and make a soup out of it the next day. I was eighteen when I finally knew what cheesecake tasted like."

He chuckled.

"And to this day I don't touch ham or turkey, not even on holidays."

"And?"

Here we go. I took a deep breath. "And a lot of stuff happened to me there."

He sat forward. His brown eyes were so comforting. He made me feel like I could put it all on the table and he would fix it.

"I've been doing this for over fourteen years. There is nothing I haven't heard, Chandria. So don't let your shame keep you from getting the help that you need."

"Well, first it started with them standing over me. Then the man who owned the group home would come into my room and force me to watch him jack off. Then he would climb under the covers and go down on me.

"By the time I had turned ten, the dad and both his sons were raping me. The dad would come to my room while everybody was asleep, carry me to the shed, and do everything imaginable you could do to a person sexually. Like I was a woman instead of a child. Then the brothers would take turns with me in the garage. One would hold me down, and the other would rape me."

He nodded. "Did you ever try to get help?"

"Yes." I laced my hands together. "I told his wife."

"What did she do?"

"Called me a liar and beat me with whatever she could get her hands on." I took a deep breath and really felt my chest open up. Telling all of this really made me feel a lot better. Like the weight was being lifted off of my chest. *Man!*

"How do you feel?" he asked me.

"Better. Not all the way, but better."

"Well, this is a start. And if we made progress the first time, imagine how much better it's going to get?"

I smiled and took in another deep breath. "Yeah."

"I'll tell you, Chandria, in all my years as a doctor, this is the first time I've ever made this much progress so fast."

"Really?"

He smiled as well. "We're going to get those demons out of you, and you'll be just fine."

I talked a little more, opening up about Onyx and how he was killed. I even told him what his friends did to me. I glanced at his clock, my time was up.

"Well, I guess I better get going. I'll see you next week." I gave him a smile as I walked to the door.

Truthfully, I wanted to stay longer and get some more stuff out. I knew I should have told him about the dreams I had been having about Dude, but I couldn't 'cause then I would've had to tell him how I knew Dude.

Chapter 15

Goldie

Red sure as hell was a slow-ass cook. The bitch was so slow, in fact, she hadn't even started cooking. And she was making tacos, of all things. Those didn't take a long damn time. Me, Cha, and Omari had been waiting at her house for the past two hours. While Omari sat in the living room watching cartoons, we all sat in Red's front yard, playing a game of dominoes on her red plastic table. Red's snake ass had managed to win again, but you never knew if her winnings were legit 'cause the bitch was so corrupt.

Just then Slow came back sweating and handed me my car keys. He was the typical crackhead: skinny, missing teeth, uncombed hair, and always dirty, uncoordinated clothes. But the muthafucka could pretty much do anything. He usually hung out in the Carmelitos doing odd jobs and had just checked my oil on my car.

"Thanks, Slow." I handed him a twenty.

He took it with his filthy fingers, nodded, and rushed away.

"Why you give him that?" Red asked. "You know he just going to smoke that shit right up."

"Because he fixed my car, dumb ass, and he always does stuff for me."

She shrugged and put her attention back on the game. "Domino!" she yelled, slamming a bone down.

"Could you domino your shit-colored ass in the kitchen and start on the tacos?" I said, holding the dominoes that threatened to fall off the table 'cause of how hard she slammed hers down.

Cha said, "Omari's hungry Red."

"I don't care bout that li'l nigga."

"What?" Cha fired.

"Playing! Relax, girl." Red stood, smoothed down her blue jean mini-skirt, and walked into the house.

Me and Cha both heard her yell, "Move, nigga!"

"Red, you better not be yelling at my baby!"

"I'm not!"

Before Cha could get up, I placed a hand on hers. "You know she playing. Red loves Omari."

"Yeah? Well, she don't show it."

"Who do the bitch show love to?" I asked. "Seriously. We her girls, and shit, but I couldn't sleep in a room with both my eyes closed with that crazy bitch, Cha."

Cha chuckled and shook her head.

"Red's a fool, but I honestly think she means well. So don't take that shit to heart."

Cha nodded.

I figured out now was a good time to tell Cha about my plans, and maybe she could join me. She had started mixing up the dominoes.

"Hey, Cha."

"Yeah."

"Have you ever thought for a second about all three of us doing something different?"

Cha had a handful of dominoes in her hand. "Different like what?"

"Different than this shit we doing now, all this hustling, tricking men, being on the system. Girl, after all my
mama had instilled in me, to see what I lowered myself to,
I know she and my daddy spinning in their grave. If I'm not
going to make something of myself, I would've been better
off going with my granny when she moved back to Georgia.
By now I could have met a Georgia man, got married, and
pushed out some kids."

Truth was, even though my grandmother didn't ad-
mit it, I felt like she blamed me for my mother's death. Her
resentment and my guilt drove me to heavy partying, drinking, and constantly running away from home with older men.

Then one day she told me straight, "I have had it
with you, Goldie. I'm selling this house, and we moving back
home to Georgia. What do you think your mother would say
if she was here?"

I shrugged in my little-ass summer dress.

"You been on the earth this long"—She snapped two
fingers together—"And you think you got all the answers. As
much as I love you, you're not going to drive me to my grave.
If you want to be out there in those streets, Goldie, I can't
stop you. Your mom taught you better. But you got a hot twat.
Can't God stop that! I found a buyer already. We are leaving
in two weeks, and if you not here 'cause you done ran your
fast ass off, I'm still boarding that plane."

Even though two years had passed, just the mention
of my mother had my eyes watery and my lips trembling.

"Come on, Goldie." She stretched her arms out for
me to step into them. "Let's go about getting past this the
right way."

I rejected her hug. I didn't think I deserved it. Instead
I ran to my room.

The day we were to leave, I was long gone, giving head to a twenty-six-year-old man I had moved in with. She did board the plane without me.

I shook my head and turned my attention back to Cha, who stared at me confused.

"Goldie, what is there to do other than this?"

Cha was serious, so I didn't call her an idiot. I spread my arms wide and smiled brightly. "Cha, there's lots of stuff. A regular job, a trade, college. We not too old or hood to go to college. What did you always wanna be when you were a kid?"

She shrugged.

"Come on negro. You always dream big as a kid."

She threw her head back and laughed. "I always wanted to be a pediatrician, you know, care for babies."

"Really? I always wanted to be a teacher."

"Yeah?"

"Yeah. Funny, as long as we known each other, we never discussed our dreams. See, we could be some bad-ass bitches. We already fine as hell. We can add *educated* and *professional* to it. Man, we would be so fly. When we graduate, we can have this big-ass party on a boat, girl. Man, we would be some cold-ass broads."

"That sounds good and all, but shit, let's be serious. Goldie, what am I going to do besides this? This is all I know. I didn't have a mama or daddy to instill shit in me. Those who could have didn't do nothing but exploit my behind. The one person who really truly loved me and made me feel like I was a part of a plan is long gone." Cha's eyes watered. She shook her head. "I'm a single parent on the county. A baby mama. I ain't got no diploma. Hell, I can barely read." She spread her arms wide. "This is me."

"What you mean, this is you?"

"This, Goldie. I'm not getting out of these walls. My only hope is that I can live to see Omari get out, live to see him go after a few dreams."

I nodded at her, feeling sad inside. Feeling sad because she really believed that shit and there was probaly nothing I could do to change that.

"You ready for another game?" she asked.

"Yeah." I placed my attention back on the game and was looking at my bones.

Cha asked me, "Who is that man by Red's car?"

I stood and shielded the sun out of my face and watched a white man open Red's car door.

"Red!" I called. "You betta get your ass out here 'fore he leave with your car, girl!"

Cha stood as well. We walked toward the dude.

By this time, I heard the screen door slam, and Red rushed out. She stood on her porch. "What?"

We both pointed at the white dude.

She bolted past us and right up to the white man. "What the fuck you doing with my car, you redneck?"

He ignored her and made an effort to get in the car.

When Red quickly blocked him from getting into the car, Cha and I stood back laughing at her crazy ass.

He said calmly, "This car has been repossessed, and I'm here to take it back to the owner."

"You ain't taking back shit muthafucka."

We couldn't hear what he said, but whatever it was made Red turn a shade of red brighter than him.

She yelled, "Oh, I'm a nigger?" and swung her balled fist at him, punching him in his nose.

When it looked like he was going to swing back, I

took a deep breath, and Cha and I rushed forward and commenced to whipping his ass. We were socking, punching, and kicking him, grabbing patches of his stringy hair.

Red scooped up a pile of dirt off the ground and threw it directly in his face.

We laughed when it flew into his eyes, mouth, and nose. He started coughing and rubbing his eyes. Cha and I slammed his face into the car.

Then he confirmed what Red had accused him of.

"Stop, niggers!"

Red growled like a pit bull and sunk her teeth into his back.

He screamed as he struggled to throw her off him. He flung his arms and knocked me off him. Then he flung the other and knocked Cha into the car.

But Red had climbed on his back and continued biting him.

I watched as blood streamed from the top of his overalls and he continued to howl at the pain, dropping to his knees like he was going to pass out.

All the while, Red pressed her face further into his back and was swinging her head from side to side.

He let out another gut-wrenching scream and dropped to the ground completely. It was only then that she pulled away and hopped off his back.

He got to his feet and took off running, but he didn't get far, tumbling in the street.

Cha and I were busting up laughing.

From the corner of my eye, I saw his blood dripping from Red's mouth.

Red took steps to go after him again, but Cha grabbed her. "Red, no."

"Move, Cha!" The look in her eyes was pure hatred.

Good thing Cha had grabbed her, 'cause we heard the sounds of a police car quickly approaching us. Police patrolled the projects daily.

As he stopped his car and hopped out, I saw he was black. *Cool.* I was hoping he would be on our side.

As the cop slowly approached us, the man stood on his feet and walked toward him. "Officer, these niggers!"

We stood and laughed, not giving a fuck about his racist ass. He deserved an ass-whipping.

The officer told him calmly, "Have a seat."

I almost had a fit. My smile dropped, and chuckles stopped, when I recognized he was the officer from the 7-Eleven. I rolled my eyes as he approached us.

"Officer, he propositioned me!" Red yelled, pointing wildly at the man, who looked like he was gonna pass out from the ass-beating.

The officer stood there and nodded, his legs spread apart, his hands behind his back. Like he was really considering Red's lies.

But then again Red was a good-ass liar.

"Officer, first he said he was going to repo my car. I asked him for the papers, and he said he didn't have any. Then he told me that he always wanted to be with a sista, and if I gave him some pussy that he would leave my car. He even said, if I gave him my number, next month he would pay my car note."

The officer raised his brows. "Is that so?"

"Yeah," we all chimed in.

That's when he noticed who I was, and his lips slipped into a smile.

I dropped my eyes.

"I told him no, officer. Then he called me an uptight nigger and slammed me on the ground. Then he spit on me! And I have two witnesses."

"Would that be you two?" he asked me and Cha.

Cha and I nodded.

He pulled a pad from behind his back and jotted down some notes. He passed me another look and then said, "Excuse me."

"Do you know him, Goldie?" Cha asked.

"No."

"Well, he acts like he know you. I'm gonna go check on Omari."

He went over to the white dude. Whatever he said to him had the white dude screaming at the top of his lungs, "You black nigger!"

The officer said, "Sir, calm down."

"Fuck you, nigger!"

Then the idiot swung on the officer, who had no choice but to lay his ass on down. He did some slick move where he grabbed one of dude's arms and twisted him so dude was lying on his stomach.

Then when the officer attempted to apply his cuffs, the dude rolled over and swung his foot at the officer's face.

The officer then took out his baton and begin fucking up dude, the whole while stating, "I am a muthafucking officer of the law."

Red got a kick out of that.

Well, I couldn't help but notice the officer's biceps, how strong he was. He applied the cuffs, lifted whitey on up, and walked him to the police car and shoved him right on in.

We walked up to the cop.

"See," Red said, "I told you, officer. He's out of control."

He kept his eyes on me and said as if he didn't really believe her, "Right. Well, I'm taking him in for booking. I'm going to need the names and number of the witnesses."

Why did he have to look pointedly at me?

"Am I free to go?" Red asked.

He nodded.

I gave him a fictitious account of what went down, to protect my nutty-ass girl.

Cha jogged back out and reiterated the same thing I said then strolled back inside.

As I turned to follow her, the po-po said, "So I finally get to know your name."

I nodded, hands on hips and eyes narrowed.

He chuckled. "Can I take you out?"

"What? Isn't this against the law?"

He bit his bottom lip. "Damn! You're beautiful."

I acted like I wasn't flattered. "What?"

"I'd just like to take you somewhere, wine and dine you, have some conversation. You think you'd like that?"

He was sexy as hell. And I liked that mouth of his. Lush. Looked like Tyrese in blue. This was too much chocolate to be walking around and for me not to get a lick, even if he was a cop. He was making my tummy flip-flop.

"Look. I know how you men in blue do, so if you think you gonna use me as project pussy you sadly mistaken officer."

He chuckled. "Project pussy."

I rolled my eyes, hands on hips.

"Why you want this?"

"I shouldn't? Why?"

"For starters, I'm a chick living in a low-income complex; you're an officer. You protect and serve." I also rob blind.

"I don't care about that. A person's environment does not necessarily define who they are. You ever killed anybody?"

"No!"

"You got good credit?"

I laughed. "A-1."

"You got a record?"

"No," I was technically telling the truth.

"Then you're dateable."

I studied him for a few moments as he leaned a knee against his patrol car and leaned his upper body forward.

"And something tells me there's more to you."

I found myself blushing. Then I immediately checked myself.

"I'm sure you'll find a way to get in contact with me," I told him, and with that, I sashayed away.

Chapter 16

Red

Now I had to find a way to get up my car note money 'cause I could hide my car for only so long. Damu told me he would easily give me two hundred if I found one of the hoes that had run away from him.

I was pissed for wasting gas searching for this dumb bitch. I looked all over Compton, LA, driving up and down Fig, then Sepulveda. I even went to the track out in Orange County by Knott's Berry Farm. I still couldn't find her ass.

I ended up finding her ass in the last place I expected to find her. In school. The bitch had quit the ho game and moved back home, trying to do right. She had shit twisted. Ain't no retiring from the ho game. Hoes damn sure didn't get no pension.

I waited outside her school. Centennial High. Once two forty-five hit, young fools escaped those gates, some stuck around. She was one of those who stuck around and was standing with a group of young bitches.

I walked toward them and kept my distance a couple feet away. "What's up, Taz?"

Her head spun my way. It was her ho name, so nobody here probably called her that.

I knew why she was his favorite, and why he was giving such a hefty fee to get her back when, for cheap, he could find one of his hoes to knock him another one. Taz was fine. Angel face, long framed lashes over gray eyes, bronze skin, full lips, and some flawless teeth. And she had titties like mangoes, a small waist, and ass to boot.

I wasn't no fool. Damu loved her. His love for her went past a pimp-ho relationship. He loved her like a man would love his wife, girlfriend, or baby mama.

It killed him that she ran away, which he went to great lengths to prevent, getting her hooked on crack cocaine to bind her to him, but still she left him.

She smiled and took a deep breath when she saw me. "Hey, Red."

As I walked toward her, she said bye to her friends. She swung her backpack over one shoulder, reached over, and hugged me.

"So what's been up with you?" I asked.

"Nothing. Back in school, trying to go at this right."

I nodded. "That's right." *Bitch, be for real. You's a ho.*

"Well, I was just checking on you to see how you were and make sure you were straight."

"I am. I'm doing good. I tried out for the cheerleading squad."

"Good." I gave her a wide smile. "You ain't gotta worry about me telling Damu. But what you think about going over to the Family Barbecue and getting a barbecue burger?"

Her face lit then just as quickly, went to disappointment. "I really should get home, Red. I have a paper I need to do."

"Girl, come on. You turning down a barbecue burger?"

She tapped her right foot on the pavement.

"It's my treat, and on top of that, I'll drop you off at home. You got my word, and you know one thing about me. I always keep it one hundred."

She laughed. "Shit! Okay. But I need to be back no later than five."

"Cool. 'Cause, girl, I could use one of them burgers."

She followed me to my car.

After we both were buckled in, I pulled onto the inter-section and drove toward Compton Blvd. I turned to her and asked, "You wanna get high?"

A look of need came, like them little starving kids in Africa. She said, "You know I don't mess with rock no more. I been clean for a month, girl. I'm getting ready to enroll in Tarzana Treatment Center. I'm on the waiting list. I'm just waiting for a bed then I'm in there."

I made a quick right then pulled into a vacant alley. I put the car in park then turned to her. "Okay, and you can get clean again. Shit! You can make your fresh start when you get to Tarzana."

"But—"

"Girl, it's Friday. Ain't nothing wrong with a little buzz." I pulled out the pipe and the little baggie with the crack in it.

She sat frozen, like she wanted to get up but couldn't bring herself to.

I loaded it up, lit it, and dangled it in front of her eyes.

"Girl, life is too short to sweat the small stuff. Every-body gets high. So, the fuck, what? Anybody got a problem with this needs to run up on me with that holier-than-thou bullshit. I got your back. I wouldn't steer you in the wrong direction, boo boo."

I pushed it toward her lips and watched her inhale it

like it was her last breath, her fingers wrapped around mine and squeezing them.

I smirked. *I got her.*

Ten minutes later, the bitch was so high, her ass couldn't even sit up straight.

Nor did she notice that I was taking her to Damu's pad on Atlantic Drive, and not Family Barbecue in Compton.

I pulled up outside and parked. I hopped out my side and rushed over to hers. Her eyes were rolling in the back of her head, and she was slouched over.

I opened her side and yanked her out. "Come on."

"We getting more?" she asked, leaning against me.

I guided her up the steps to his place. I walked behind her, one hand in the small of her back.

When we got to the top step, she almost fell back.

I held her up. "Stop acting stupid and walk!" I yelled.

She giggled. "Sorry. Need another hit. Is this the dope spot?"

"Sure is," I lied. The bitch was too high to even see straight.

"Cooooool."

"Walk!"

"I can't. I'm blasted."

I assisted her ass to apartment 216 and knocked quickly. As she crouched near me, I snatched her up.

I heard a deep voice say, "Come in."

I turned the knob and pushed the door open enough to shove her inside. Then I stepped inside to see Damu seated on the couch, facing us. I stood calmly while she stumbled over her own feet.

She blinked a couple times. I guess, she was starting to come down from her high.

She stood up erect now, her whole body trembling. "Is that . . .?"

Poor thing! Oh, fucking, well. "Here this crack fien', Damu."

He didn't say shit. She didn't say shit neither. Tears were slipping from her eyelids.

I was sure he was gonna, at least, slap the shit out of her. I didn't feel like seeing him beat her ass. I just wanted to get my dough and bounce.

But Damu surprised me when he stood to his feet and pulled out a gun from the waistband of his pants. He aimed it at her head and blew the back of it clear off.

Chapter 17

Cha

I had that dream again. This was the third time this happened this week and today was only Wednesday. I stared down at Omari's face. He was sleeping so peacefully.

I grabbed my purse off the floor and rummaged through it. It was a cheap one I had grabbed at the Compton Swap Meet after I'd left my purse along with all my stuff at Dude's house, which scared the mess out of me because my ID was in it. But, still, it didn't seem like he suspected that I was part of that robbery.

I found my doctor's card. He'd told me feel free to call him whenever the need hit me, whenever I needed to talk. I sure hope he meant that 'cause it was one in the morning and I desperately needed to talk to him.

I dialed his number and took a deep breath. He sounded groggy when he answered.

"Hi, Doctor Baker. It's me, Cha. Chandria. Ummm, you said I could call you if I needed to talk."

"Yes, I did. How are you, Chandria?"

"I'm not too good."

"Why not?"

"I been having this dream for the past week."

"Oh."

"To be honest, I'm a little scared to say what the dream was about."

"Why is that?"

I licked my dry lips. I gazed at Omari. His lips were poked out and he was breathing through his mouth. I smiled and rubbed my fingers over his curly hair.

"You know my son is the most important thing in my life. And I know what people say about girls who have kids and live in the projects, but what they say is not always true. See, I don't mind working. It's just that, after what I been through it's hard for me to trust my son with anybody. So that's always been my fear. That if I put him in the care of another, someone will do to him what was done to me." I swallowed hard. "The only person I feel safe with my son being with is my neighbor. She keeps him for me. But she can't do too much 'cause she got five of her own she takes care of by herself. And you know what else? I was gonna get a fast-food job, graveyard shift. I interviewed for it and everything, even got hired. But according to the guidelines here I may have to move 'cause, combined with my welfare, I'd make too much. Then there's a chance they could cut me off of that too. And on my own I'd never make it. I need assistance. So when they called and offered me the job last week, I didn't take it."

"How much would you have been making?"

"Thirteen hundred a month."

"I see."

I chuckled. "But you know what. That's not even why I called you. I called you 'cause of the dreams I've been having."

"How long have you been having them?"

"For the past two years. Ever since my kid's father was killed. It's the real reason why I started seeing you, 'cause seems like I have them darn near every night now. I have a hard time getting to sleep.

"But the dreams changed. Someone is always getting raped or molested. I can see it all from a picture window, but I can't get in the house." I took a deep breath. "The doors are locked and the window won't break. The same"—My voice cracked. I shook my head and felt the tears coming—"The same people raping the boy were the same men who raped me when I was a kid." I wiped my tears away. "But that's not the only thing about the nightmare that bothers me. The little boy in the house is my son, Omari."

"I see. You know during our last session you know what I was thinking?"

"What?"

"How could someone hurt such a beautiful woman?"

"Maybe beauty is a curse," I mumbled. "Mine never did nothing for me."

"Not with me."

My eyes narrowed.

"I hope you don't object to me saying this, but you are the sexiest woman I have ever seen."

"What?" I could barely get it out.

"Since you said you can't sleep, what are you going to be doing for the next couple of hours? I'll pay for a babysitter."

I gasped and slammed the phone down, waking Omari out of his sleep.

Chapter 18

Goldie

I didn't know if I should do this. I felt like I was hanging with the enemy. My mama was probably flipping in her grave. I sighed and stepped out of the shower.

I heard someone at my goddamn door. I opened it, wondering who the hell it was.

It was a black delivery guy with a medium-sized box. He was lushing on my curves in my little robe. "Godiva Hangel?"

I nodded.

"Sign here." He handed me a pen to scribble across a strip of paper that he later ripped off the package.

I was curious as to what it was and from whom. Regardless, I was going to keep it.

I slammed the door shut before he could spit some punk game and tore the box open. Inside was a white linen dress. It was pretty but not my style, which was low-rider jeans that exposed my tat that said, "Trust no dick," and the tips of my ample ass, and tank tops.

Still curious how it would drape my body, I slipped off my robe and pulled it on. And I'll tell you what, it felt good as hell against my skin. The top hung like a sheath and crisscrossed my tummy, exposing my belly button, and the rest hung to my ankles in slits. Made me feel sexy and womanly at the same time.

I figured out it was from the officer. I piled my weave up on my head as best I could, so my tracks didn't show, and slid my feet in some simple flip-flops with a heel. I put on some baby oil and strawberry daiquiri-scented perfume, and was all done.

I didn't even give Rick a chance to get out of his car as he pulled up. I tossed a five to Slow for waxing my ride. That was all I had. Then I marched straight to the passenger side. No, sir. You offer a date a free meal, you wasn't getting no cookies as an appetizer. But he still hopped out as I made a quick move to open the passenger door.

When I noticed he wouldn't stop staring, I snarled, "Why the fuck are you looking at me?"

"'Cause you look pretty."

Rick was dressed like a regular dude, a simple sweater, some slacks. *Gators?* He slid between the car door and me and opened my side for me. I slid in, exposing a lot of thigh.

To be honest, I didn't want to go to this restaurant the Churrascaria in Beverly Hills. I never had Brazilian food. What if I made a fucking fool of myself?

"I'd much rather go to the pier."

"Which one?" he asked as he drove out of the Carmelitos.

"Santa Monica."

"Okay."

I studied his profile. He was fine as hell.

Once we made it to the pier, we had to damn near fight our way through the crowd. "Damn," I muttered.

He laughed and curled one hand around my waist, even though I never gave him permission.

We went over to the side of the pier where people were

fishing and there was a dude doing tricks. Couples leaned over the pier and stared into the water.

"You want to see the show baby?" He gestured toward the dude doing tricks and begging for money.

"Hell, no. I don't want to see his lame-ass."

Rick chuckled.

Wanting to feel like all the happy little couples, I leaned against the railing staring down. It wasn't any view because the water was dirty as fuck. I turned my head to get a look at Rick.

"You know they say there are places you can go and the water is so clear, you can see your feet in it. And they say the sand is as white as milk."

I closed my eyes, imagining it. "Man, I would love to go there."

Rick stood directly behind me, slipping closer and closer.

"Hey, homeboy. What are you doing?"

He chuckled near my ear and kissed the tip of my ear. "I thought we were having a moment."

I laughed. "*I* was having a moment, officer."

He chuckled. "Here we go with this shit again."

"Shit? Ouuu! You curse?"

"I am by no means perfect."

I spun around to face him. "Let's hear it."

"I grew up in LA."

"Your hood?"

"Athens Park."

"Oh, shit." I knew all about that gang. They were notorious for kicking up shit. "You gangbanged?"

Rick pulled up his shirt and exposed an APB tat on his upper arm.

"I can't believe you banged."

"Well, you live and you learn."

"Ever killed anybody?"

"Naw, just bust some asses in my day, messed with the honeys. I smoked so much weed, I'm still high to this day."

I had a vision of him in a wife-beater, some baggy jeans, and a du-rag. The image got me a little wet in the panties. *Humph.* So he was a dude with an edge to him.

"Anyway, I got thrown in juvie, talked to staff, changed my perspective, and I been right ever since. Traded in my gang for the force."

"You sound so corny saying that."

He chuckled then reached down and hugged me.

"You know you a little too touchy-feely, officer. You might wanna control that." Honestly, I didn't mind one bit. It felt wholesome, so I didn't fight him one bit. I liked it, and I liked him.

Rick leaned down and whispered in my ear, "I can't help it, beautiful." He kissed my lips softly.

I pulled away. "Ex-thug using the word *beautiful.*"

"It's the only word I can use to describe you."

He gripped me tighter. "So anything you wanna share with me?"

"Nope. Nothing 'cept—"

"'Cept what?"

"I'm a hustler."

"Damn."

We both burst out laughing.

Chapter 19

Cha

Maybe it was a bad idea for me to turn that job down. Well, my neighbor thought so.

"Girl, don't trip," she told me. "I will watch Omari for you. And you know he is going to be safe with me. I will guard that cute little nigga with my life."

I smiled at her. She had me when Onyx was alive and used to look out for her and her kids. We knew she struggled, especially after the county passed that rule a few years ago that even if you had more kids they were not going to increase your cash aid, so we always gave her extra cash. When she couldn't make a way for them, we did, hooking them up every Christmas and during their birthdays.

"Go on and take that job, girl. You never know. You may end up being a manager one day and moving out of this hellhole."

So I did. I started off slow, though, only working thirty hours a week. And it turned out I didn't get graveyard shift, I worked during the day. My worker told me I could stay on the county as long as I stayed under thirty hours. That way I'd get to keep my health benefits and low-income housing. And, yes, I was only working at Taco Bell, but still I felt a sense of pride. I was now a working mother. I knew if Onyx could see me, he would be proud. Within two days I learned the cash register and how to wrap the packaging on the items on the menu.

The only annoying thing about working there was, my male coworkers were always making passes at me, brushing up against me, or asking me for my number.

I shut them down quickly, saying, "You can't have it 'cause it's not on the menu."

When giving attitude made them chase after me even more, I tried to be as plain as possible, no makeup, a hat on my head, and I wore my pants two sizes too big. Then I went to a 99-cent store and found a silver band that I slipped on my ring finger, but that didn't help. The only one who kept it somewhat professional with me was my shift manager, Solomon. His expression was serious with me, and his conversation always work-related. But the supervisor was a mess.

I worked from 6 A.M. to 12 P.M. and still had plenty of time to spend with Omari, even cook dinner and go to the park. I had extra cash, half of which I gave to my neighbor for watching Omari.

My favorite part about working there was being able to work the drive-thru. After a month I was no longer considered a new booty, and I was working the window like a vet. I didn't get annoyed by crazy customers either.

Tonight I was covering for my coworker.

"I held the button on the intercom and spoke into the microphone.

"Welcome to Taco Bell. May I take your order?"

"I'll take some fried chicken, red beans and rice, and . . ."

Fried chicken, red beans, and rice? Does this chick know where she is? "I'm sorry, ma'am. We don't serve those items."

"What, bitch? You mean I can't get no muthafucking red beans and rice?"

Before I could respond, I heard, "Red, shut the fuck up! You might get our girl in trouble. What's up, baby? This is Goldie. Give us four of those seventy nine cent waters and two ice waters. Sorry. We on a budget."

I smiled and give them the total.

My coworker working the line was looking at me like I was crazy.

Red's dumb behind screamed out, "My red beans and rice!"

I stifled a giggle and waited for them to pull up to the window.

"What up, nigga?" Red said, her head hanging out of the car.

I shook my head at her and snatched the money. "You stupid, Red!"

Goldie exclaimed, "Look at Cha. I'm so proud of you."

I punched the amount in the cash register and grabbed their change and receipt. I handed it to Red.

"We going out tonight. You wanna roll?" Goldie asked leaning over in her seat to see me in the drive thru window.

I shook my head. "Naw. I'll be too tired. Plus I promised Omari breakfast at IHOP tomorrow."

I grabbed their bag of food and the two ice waters. I then handed it all to Red while she talked her mess.

"Oh, so, bitch, you get you a little job, and you think you too good to be seen with us? Hand me some hot sauce!"

I grabbed several hot sauces from the bin and handed them to her.

She looked at them and shouted, "Bitch, I need mild!"

"Well, you said hot sauce dumb ass," Goldie said.

I grabbed a handful of mild and threw them at her.

Goldie busted up laughing.

"Y'all go before y'all get me fired."

As they pulled off, Red yelled while tossing a fist out the window, "My red beans and rice!"

Chapter 20

Red

"On the real, y'all, I don't know why they call ya'll hoes. Shit! They the ones making all the dough. Really, to me, y'all should be called the pimps."

I stared across from these three young, pretty bitches, hoping they bought my "drag."

One thing was for sure. I was cool on Damu's ass. After he killed that bitch, I decided to part ways with him. I didn't need to get caught up in no shit for a damn pimp. Now I was working for Harem. So far I had managed to steal six of Damu's hoes away.

I used slick talk. "Why you wanna work for Damu's lame-ass? Harem take better care of his hoes, and you rarely on the stroll. He got private customers calling, and shit. He will treat y'all hoes like you high-class even if you ain't. And lets face it. Y'all raggedly bitches ain't."

That was all it took. They left Damu's ass high and dry except for his bottom bitch Scarlet. She shook her head at me and said, "Red, you one cutthroat bitch."

"Yeah. And in a few months your loose-ass pussy is going to hit the concrete so you better pick a trade bitch."

That got her hot. "Fuck you "And if its anything that's gonna hit the concrete its my feet bitch 'cause I stay taking these nigga's money."

"Bitch you busted. You ain't making no money."

I turned to walk away when I heard her say.

"I'll be sure to let Damu know who responsible for taking his hoes," she warned. "And you better believe he will be coming for your ass 'cause you fucking with his pockets."

I started to fuck her up for threatening me but I thought smarter and left. What proof did she have?

For every ho I put on Harem's payroll, shit, I was banking two hundred. And after I passed them six over, I got more ambitious and slick. I didn't have time to try to convince hoes who were fucked in, over, and out, and set in their ways, to go get put on Harem's payroll.

Now I was recruiting teenyboppers to get cracked. The most fucked up and damaged ones made the best recruits, since they had such low self-esteem. You show these dumb pigs thirty seconds of attention and you could do just about anything to them, and they wasn't going nowhere. The best places to find them were at abortion clinics, nearby burger joints, sitting outside school, hanging in the projects and parks. They were usually just sitting around looking like a fucking lost puppy, in some boy's laps, or running with a little crew.

"Girls, I'm telling y'all, this nickel-and-dime bullshit out here ain't cutting it. Bush is fucking this country up, and they ain't about to put no nigga in the White House. We as women got to embrace the feminine movement and stack our own damn dough."

All three girls looked at me like I was a light-skin Sister Souljah.

One of them was Taffy. She had caramel-colored skin, doe eyes, a mole on the side of her face, and a slender body with bow legs. She was fourteen.

April was chocolate, with cat eyes, and wore her thick hair in a puffy ponytail on the top of her head. The girl had a small waist and way too much ass for a thirteen-year-old.

Cola was a red bone like me, with curly hair, perky titties, and big thighs and hips. I just wondered how in the hell a twelve-year-old got the nickname *Cola*. Well, I didn't really care.

"So let's have it. What's y'all take on this, girls? Y'all ain't never exchanged anything for money before?"

"You mean sex?" Cola asked.

I nodded.

"Well, my daddy gives me five bucks a week if I let him stick his fingers in me when my mama gone."

"Humph," April snorted. "My stepdad puts his dick in my pussy all the time, and he don't give me nothing for it. My mama don't believe me no way, so I stop fighting him and let him take it."

"Ain't that some shit!" I said, pumping her up.

"What 'bout you, Taffy?"

She dropped her eyes. "Well, when my mom want some of that stuff, she gets me dressed up and makes me go over to that dope spot in apartment fifteen and let the dope man do stuff to me."

"And what the fuck do you get?" Red asked.

"I get two rocks to give to my mama."

Damn! They all fucked up! Perfect! "See what the fuck I'm saying! Y'all sell your bodies for everybody but yourself. Get your own money and stuff. I'm talking about getting your nails and hair done, True Religion jeans, a Coach, or Dooney & Bourke bag. Y'all young girls like that stuff. You should be able to eat good in places like this," I said, gesturing around Hometown Buffet.

"Harem is the dude for y'all. The niggas got so many connections, yesterday one girl said she went on a date with Chris Brown."

At the mention of his name, their eyes bucked. April looked like she was creaming in her panties.

But I was lying my ass off.

"Let's just go meet him, and y'all can say, 'Red, I'm cool,' or 'Red, I'm *cool.* I just don't like to see my young sistas going out like that. I want to see y'all accomplish something in this sorry-ass world."

Cola, the youngest of the three said, "It don't sound bad to me."

"Well, finish eating, so we can roll by Harem's crib and you can meet him personally."

Fifteen minutes later, we boned out, in my ride to Harem's house. Harem had the game right, and was about his money. This nigga didn't live in no apartment building. He lived in this big-ass house on Atlantic on the east side of Long Beach and had hoes working on multiple strolls like Damu, Pacific Coast Highway, Long Beach Boulevard, and Artesia. He threw the tow-up bitches on Fig in LA.

These dumb hoes were blasting Amanda Perez's "God Send Me an Angel," and getting on my muthafucking nerves. Wasn't nobody sending these dumb bitches no angel. And Amanda was probably somewhere getting high, fucked, or something.

"You got some Keyshia Cole, Red?" Taffy asked.

"No," I lied. *You not listening to my shit.* "We here any-how, girls." I put my car in park and turned off the ignition.

"He live in this pad, Red?" Cola asked.

"Yeah, girl, he ballin'. He could probably show you how to get a pad like this."

They fast asses followed me up to the door.

After I knocked, Cherry, one of Harem's hoes opened the door. The bitch wasn't but seventeen, but sucking dick and fucking since you was eleven had a way of making you feel grown.

She had skin the color of caramel, chinky eyes, silky hair, and big dick-sucking lips. Her body was out of this world. And she rode so much dick, she had a permanent gap between her legs.

"What's up, Red? You brought us some wifeys to get cracked?"

"We'll see. What you think? They got potential? You think Harem gonna like them?"

Her eyes scanned all three of the girls. Funny, all looked nervous except for the twelve-year-old. Her mama sure fucked her up.

"They got the potential to be some fly-ass bitches, no doubt." Cherry stepped aside. "Come on in, y'all."

I followed after the girls and scanned his lavish-ass house. *Damn! If I were a man, I sure would pimp some hoes.*

"Follow me, girls. Red, you too. Harem want to holla at you."

We walked past the living room, where some hoes were lounging, to the spiral staircase.

Once we got to Harem's room, Cherry knocked.

"Come in."

"Daddy, Red bought you a couple of"—Cherry glanced back at the three girls and giggled—"treats."

"Send them in. Tell Red I will be with her in a few."

She turned back to us. "Go on in girls. Red, you can go back downstairs and wait in the living room. You want some Henny?"

I leaned back against the wall as the girls entered. I knew one thing. I wasn't leaving until I got my cash. "I'm straight, but I'll wait downstairs."

"Cool."

The door was closed in my face abruptly, so I marched my ass downstairs and sat on one of the couches. *Damn! What the fuck did he have to do? Examine them like he was a gynecologist? The nigga was taking shit too far. Give them bitches some outfits and throw them out on the track.*

I sat there impatiently and skimmed a *Vibe* magazine. I was reading a Jay-Z interview and halfway done when Cherry came bouncing down the stairs, giggling and flustered.

"Harem wants to talk to you."

I followed her ass up them damn stairs again.

Cherry kept on giggling, getting on my fucking nerves. Why the fuck wasn't her ass on the track? What was this, her day off? I didn't know hoes had days off.

She knocked on the door.

Calmly he said, "Enter."

I walked in the room quickly, my view blocked by Cherry's big ass. When she moved out of the way, I damn near passed out.

Harem was sitting in the big-ass chair like he was the king of France while Taffy was ass buck-naked, booty tooted up in the air, and bobbing her head up and down on his dick.

I heard heavy breathing coming from the right. Cola was on her knees, leaning over a coffee table and snorting up lines of coke like she was a human vacuum cleaner. And April was behind her, gripping her thighs and eating her pussy like she was a pro.

Now I done seen some shit, but nothing like this. By the way Cola was sniffing that powder and April was digging out that pussy, I would say they got turned out in a matter of seconds.

Harem calmly counted out six hundred-dollar bills and passed them to Cherry, who was now dressed down to a thong and a lacy bra. She walked over to me and placed the money in my hands.

"I'll be calling you soon, Red," Harem said. Then he gripped the back of Taffy's head and shoved it down further on his dick.

I nodded, threw up the peace sign, and walked to the door.

Cherry followed after me, but before she could shut the door, I heard Harem say, "Cherry, show her how to suck a dick right."

Chapter 21

Cha

Man, it felt good to get a check you worked for. I had been at Taco Bell for exactly four months now. Felt good. I would come home in my uniform stinky and proud as heck.

Another perk from working for Taco Bell, I was able to get leftovers. I didn't bring too much home because I didn't want Omari to get hooked on junk food and not want to eat his vegetables anymore. So I toted the leftovers to my neighbor's house. And her kids would gobble it up.

I was thinking about increasing my hours. Maybe then I could get off the county.

The area supervisor kept saying I had the potential to be a manager, but when he said that, it was always after undressing me with his eyes. I ignored his behind, though. I wasn't about to mix business with pleasure. And I wasn't ready to date anyone anyhow.

He would give me long breaks, bring me back lunch, even gave me overtime money on my check. All this crap was nice, but I didn't want any favors that I would have to return.

Pay day fell on my off day, so I went up there to get my check and talk to my supervisor. I was sure he would leave me alone if I checked his behind.

And if I had the guts to check my boss, maybe, just

maybe, I'd have the guts to check my doctor for that mess he'd said to me. 'Cause, Lord knows, I needed to start my counseling again. I mean having this job made me feel so good about myself. But still . . . I had baggage I needed to get rid of. Most importantly, I was having those dreams again. Only, I wasn't as worried as I was before about them because this time it wasn't about my baby. The dreams were now about me.

"Hey," I said to Solomon. He was standing behind the register.

He nodded.

"Is the sup here?"

"Yeah, he's in his office."

I walked past the register to the back of the restaurant. I ignored another male staff grunting at me. My supervisor's office door was open, but I knocked on it anyway.

His head popped up and he said, "Come in, Cha."

I walked inside.

Ronald wasn't an ugly man. In fact, he was actually cute and resembled Matthew McConaughey a little. Sandy blond hair with blue eyes, he was a preppy-looking white man that liked to dip into a sista or two, never mind the shiny wedding band on his finger.

He passed my check to me, and the form to sign. I did so quickly and opened my check and scanned it. He had added twenty hours of overtime, so my check was way over the amount my sixty hours amounted to.

"Look, Mr. Brown, I appreciate this. I really do. But I wish you would stop doing all this extra stuff."

He leaned back in his chair. "Why, Cha?"

"Because I don't have anything extra to give you. And because I'm not giving you anything extra." I raised a brow, so he'd get the point.

"Cha, I just think you are a very beautiful woman." His eyes scanned my curves.

"Look, sir, I'm just here to do my six hours a day, and that's it. Please leave—"

"I know you have a son. I can take care of you. You wouldn't have to work or do anything."

"I don't need you to, sir."

He smiled and bit his bottom lip. "Why are you making this so hard?"

What? Has no one ever told him no?

"I wouldn't hurt you. I'd be very good to you. And, to tell you the truth, all your rejection is doing is making me more interested."

"I'm not interested. I would like all of this to stop."

He stared at me for a moment before saying. "Okay. Sorry."

"Thank you. And when I cash my check, I will refund the extra money that—"

"No. Keep it. Consider it a bonus for all the hard work you do. Buy your son a gift."

I smiled and walked out the door. But I was still going to give it right back to him.

Chapter 22

Red

I was supposed to go out and find some more hoes for Harem but didn't really feel like it. I smiled and watched my neighbor rush up the steps to her apartment with her three pigs in tow. I listened to her ask them how their day at school went. *Does she really give a damn?* The bitch and her offspring got on my nerves. She was pretty though. Brown skin. Coca-Cola shape . . . after three fucking kids. She even had pretty feet.

Although I normally watched her day to day, the truth was, I didn't like her or her kids. I always turned my nose up at her piglets, always coming to my door to borrow flour and shit. She worked long hours during the graveyard shift, and since her dumb ass couldn't afford childcare, her eight-year-old watched the four and three-year-old.

Single parent. Waa! Waa! Waa! Who gives a fuck? If you want shit, better hustle.

Then an idea hit me. Why not proposition her ass? She'd be a fool to turn it down.

I walked out my door and approached her apartment. I knocked.

She opened her door after the second knock and was surprised as hell to see me on her doorstep.

"Hey, girl," I chimed in a cheerful cheerleader smile. I knew my eyes were hooded from the weed I had just smoked.

"Hello," she said quietly.

She was probably still pissed from our last encounter, when her youngest son came to my door to borrow some milk. After a few words from me he ran away crying and the next thing I know, here comes her angry ass bamming on my door.

"What the fuck you want?"

"Did you call my son a project bastard?" she demanded.

"No, I didn't call that bastard nothing."

Her eyes got wide but before she could respond I slammed the door in her face.

But today my approach was more friendly. "Listen, I want to squash the beef, since we neighbors and all."

Without hesitation, she said, "Oh, okay, girl," her smile was warm, genuine.

"Girl, I see how you struggling and all, so I have a way for you to make some quick cash."

Her eyes perked up, like I figured they would. Hell, it was almost December.

"Girl, you do?"

I nodded.

"I sure could use some extra cash. What you need? Your house cleaned?"

I shook my head. "I work for a dude name Harem. He networks out here, so I could put you on."

"Put me on what?" she asked with narrowed eyes.

I had to spell it out to this bitch. "Selling pussy and head."

She waved her hand and laughed. "Are you for real?"

I nodded.

"Do you see me and my kids going to church every Sunday?"

"Save that eye-on-the-sparrow shit, bitch! You got three kids that don't look alike, and no husband."

She stepped closer until she was all up in my face. "You sick bitch! Get off my steps!"

Bitch? My head snapped back in shock, my high fucked off. She had the game twisted.

I balled up my fist, but just as quickly unballed it when an officer patrolled on by us. It was Rick's ass. I smiled at her and backed away.

"I'm gonna fuck your world up just because," I growled.

She shook her head at me. "I truly feel sorry for you."

I marched back to my house and slammed my door shut. I went in search of my phonebook. I found it and thumbed through the pages until I found the number for DCFS.

Chapter 23

Goldie

I was getting closer and closer to Rick. That one date turned into three, and now I was doing something I couldn't have imagined. I was on a damn plane nibbling on shrimp cocktail next to him on my way to Tahiti. I was eating only out of nerves because my black ass had never been on an airplane. The closest I ever got to flying was when I was high on Indigo weed.

Before we got a chance to relax, I was already out of my clothes and into a hot pink bikini so I could go frolic on the beach. I slammed out of the bathroom, grabbed a towel, and slipped my feet into some flip-flops.

"You better throw your ass in some trunks 'cause I'm not going to waste my time in this room," I told Rick. "I'll be on the beach."

I was almost out the door when I felt his hand wrap around my waist. He had no comment about my mouth.

Man, I could be such a bitch. I promised myself quietly that I would be nice to him for the rest of the trip. Well, hell, I'd try to.

I spun around in his arms and gave him a hug.

Rick gripped his hands underneath my thighs, flung me over his shoulder, and carried me through the hotel. I giggled, the whole while having a ball, but still yelling, "Boy, put my ass down!"

He slapped my rump. "Hush up, girl."

Ouuu. That shit made my coochie flip-flop. So he wasn't a pushover. "Girl? I'm a grown-ass woman, dawg."

As he continued to walk, I felt a gust of wind against my bottom. Then all of a sudden, he stopped walking and slid my body down his.

"Turn around, baby."

I did, and that's when I saw it! The water. It was beautiful, unlike anything I had ever seen before.

I splashed through it and couldn't help but look back at Rick, who just looked at me with a smile on his sexy face. I still couldn't believe that he invited me to a place like this. I felt special. Yeah, I hadn't have any man make me feel that way. Ever.

I giggled as he made his way toward me. You know I had to play that role at least once before I died. Shit! The one where you are in the water screaming, running from a dude, while he chases you. Then he catches you, and y'all both fall in the water. I was having so much fun, I didn't care my weave got wet. I had a perm on my edges anyhow.

I let him grab my hand and pull me out of the water, and we walked on the sand. I followed him to some straw lounge chairs. I lay on my back and allowed him to dry me off.

"Turn over, baby."

I sucked in a deep breath as he gently rubbed the towel up my calves, to my thighs, and damn, he stopped a few inches from my pussy. But it still turned me the fuck on.

When it was his turn, I wasted no time touching that golden sun-kissed body of his. I worked my hands down his arms, chest, and down his legs. Then my eyes went to his bulge. Yeah, dude was packing.

He snatched the towel from me and threw it on the chair. Then he pulled me in his arms. "Have you ever ridden in a hot air balloon, baby?"

I shook my head excitedly. "Are we going to go get on one?"

He gripped my waist tighter and kissed me. He continued to kiss me all the way to the hot air balloon.

The next thing I knew we were floating in the sky. That shit was the muthafucking bomb, I screeched.

Rick watched my expression and wrapped his arms around my waist. "You having fun, baby?"

"Yes. I'm having so much fun."

"Good."

"What do you want to do next?"

Chapter 24

Cha

I was busy mopping the dining hall floor. I was supposed to be off at six. My plans were to go pick up some movies, a pizza, and hang with Omari. Only, my relief didn't show up, so I had to stay until closing.

Now, more than ever, Red was mad because I wouldn't hang with her, and Goldie didn't care because she was always with her cop boyfriend.

Business was so slow that night. There was only me and another female cashier, but since she cooked the food I was the only one on the floor.

Ronald walked out of his office, briefcase in hand, and came toward me.

"You know what, Chandria, you work entirely too hard."

I stopped mopping when he placed one of his hands over mine. I looked back to see if the cook was in sight, but she wasn't.

Ronald raised my chin up, so I was looking at him. "Why don't you leave with me? We can go for drinks and get some ceviche. You ever had ceviche before?"

I narrowed my eyes. "Ce-what?"

He chuckled. "It's crab and shrimp in a lemon sauce.

It's really good. Or we can go somewhere you like. Come with me. I'll cover for you. You'll still get paid."

I pulled away. "Sir, I already told you. I'm not interested."

"Aww, come on." He placed a hand around my waist. "Your waist is so tiny."

I gently peeled his hand off of me.

He slid a piece of paper to me. "Here is my cell. If you change your mind, call me, Cha. I will be up. I'm like a night owl." He winked at me and walked out the door.

I shook my head as he skidded out of the parking lot in his E-Class Benz.

Leticia, the other cashier on duty, rushed out. "Is he gone?"

I nodded.

"I got a party to go to. I'm sneaking out. Can you drop the deposit off at the bank, Cha? I was supposed to do it earlier, but I forgot. They're closed inside, but they have a drop box."

I shrugged. "Okay." I wheeled my cart away back to the storage room.

"Thanks, Cha. It's on Ronald's desk in the blue satchel bag."

"Lock the door on your way out!" I yelled.

I shoved the cart in the room. I flicked it right back off, closed the door back, and locked it. As I was about to turn back around and head back out to the dining hall, I felt something press into my side, making every hair on my body stand.

"The bitch forgot to lock the door, but don't worry, when I finish what I'm doing, I won't forget to lock it, baby."

The voice almost made me pee in my panties. It was Dude! I held my breath.

His eyes bore into me. "You lied. You stole from me, bitch. I'm getting two things, one my money that you stole, and since I lost so much and never got it, that pussy." He shoved a gun to my head.

"Please."

He grabbed me by my hair and forced me to follow him.

Whimpering, I did what he said, and the store went completely black.

"Where is it?"

"What?"

He gripped my neck. "Look, bitch, I don't want to ruin your pretty face before I fuck you, so don't play that game with me. The bitch gave you the money to deposit to the bank. That's what I want. Now!"

Oh God! He must've been casing the place and watching me. I wonder for how long? Why did I promise to take the money to the bank?

I made my way in the dark to the office with Dude close on my heels. My heart was racing, and tears were running down my face. I'm sure there had to be at least $4,000 in that pouch. I slipped on the light in the room and saw it on the desk. I handed it to him without looking at him, my hands shaking.

I knew what was next and tried to mentally prepare myself for it.

He tucked it in his baggy jeans. "Take off your clothes!"

I didn't question or beg. I knew he was going to rape me. I kept my eyes open because if I closed them, I would see images of hands all over me, a penis shoved in my mouth, fingers prodding me.

I unbuttoned my work shirt, pulled it off, slipped off my shoes, unbuckled my belt and let my pants drop.

Before I could get to my bra, he pointed the gun at me. "Come here." He was now leaning against Ronald's desk.

I walked toward him, and he reached out and grabbed me by my butt, so that I straddled him.

"You so pretty," he said gently. "I wanted to make you my woman." Then he pressed the cold steel of the gun against my heart. "But you had to be a bitch and set me up!"

I closed my eyes briefly and saw images of myself as a ten-year-old with semen spilling on my face. I opened them quickly.

Dude ripped my bra off, and my breasts spilled out. Then he used the gun to slide my panties off. He gripped the back of my head and kissed me so rough, I could barely breathe, and his teeth nicked the inside of my mouth.

Then he started playing inside of me with his fingers. Two, three. Cruelly deep. He rubbed the steel of the gun against my clit.

I was dying inside.

He shoved me to my knees. "I'm getting it all from you tonight—some head, pussy, and ass." He shoved his dick in my mouth.

I did my best to do what he wanted.

After a while he shoved me to the floor and covered my body with his. He slid on a condom and gripped my thighs in his hands.

I kept my eyes opened to avoid seeing the same images, but keeping them open gave me no choice but to look into his eyes, which bore into mine as he violated me. He wasn't vicious, but because I was dry, I felt like my skin was tearing. I kept quiet though.

I felt his fingers digging into my thighs, heard him huffing and puffing. His eyes looked so devilish. "I'm so sorry," I whispered.

"Shut up, bitch!" He gripped my throat.

I nodded, tears sliding down my cheeks.

When he flipped me over, I knew what was next.

I placed my hands over my mouth and bit one of my fingers so hard, I drew blood from the pain of him pumping me in and out of my butt like it was my coochie.

He gripped me and continued to ride me. I just prayed it would be over soon. Kept asking myself, *Could I blame him?* I had done him wrong.

He let out a series of groans and started slapping my behind with each stroke.

I bit down on another finger.

When I felt his pace picking up and he let out a series of shudders, each one more agitated, I knew he was done.

He shoved me off him and threw the condom on the floor. He started putting on his jeans, while I stayed frozen.

"I would have been good to you, Jade. Part of me still wants to."

I turned over and looked at him. I don't know why, but I did.

His face got tender, like he wanted to wrap me in his arms but wouldn't allow himself to. Then he backed out of the restaurant.

Seconds later I heard a car screech down the street, leaving me to deal with the mess I had made.

Chapter 25

Red

My sneaky ass watched from my window, puffing on a blunt with some chronic inside of it, as the police tore her apartment apart. I heard screaming and crying.

I fell on the couch laughing as they walked her stuck-up ass out in handcuffs and shoved her in the squad car. Then her little pigs were next.

I figured the lady that arrived with the cops was a social worker because they forced the kids kicking and screaming into her car.

Damn! They move fast. I took in a long puff as they drove away and reflected on what I did just yesterday. I cased her pad and waited 'till the *biatch* went to work. Then I knocked on her door, equipped with a bag of Doritos, a tub of ice cream, and some licorice.

The youngest boy opened the door.

"Hi."

"Hi." He looked at me innocently, blocking the doorway.

"Your mom didn't tell you I was coming?"

He shook his head.

"Well, you know she be busy. It probably slipped her mind. I brought some ice cream, candy, and chips for y'all."

"My big brother ain't here. He snuck out to play with his friends and left me and Angel home alone, so he don't deserve no ice cream."

What a hater.

"Well, you can eat his share. How that sound?"

His face brightened up.

"Now, if you don't let me in, the ice cream will melt, li'l man."

He moved aside, and I slipped in.

"Here. Put it in the kitchen."

Once he walked away, I searched for their mother's room. In the first room the daughter was napping on a bunk bed, so I knew that wasn't it. I slipped out and went to the opposite door across from that room. *Jackpot.*

I rushed up to her raggedy dresser. I opened it and laid a pipe, a bag of crack, and some weed on a pair of her underwear. Then I slipped out. I didn't have time to critique her piece-of-shit pad.

I peeked in the kitchen. The little boy had climbed on their kitchen table to put the ice cream away.

He saw me and yelled, "Bye."

I flipped him the bird and was out the door.

Seeing the cops and social worker was confirmation that my plan had worked because that ho was going to the slammer.

Chapter 26

Cha

"So you mean to tell me that four thousand dollars is gone?"

I stared at Ronald, who was leaned back in his chair, studying me. I nodded.

"How the hell could this happen?" Before I could answer, he said, "Wait. I'm asking the wrong person. I should be talking to Leticia. The drop was her responsibility. She should have deposited it yesterday morning, not wait until the last minute. But how can I be convinced you didn't drag in one of your hoodlum buddies to rob us, Chandria?"

I didn't answer. Didn't think it would really matter if I did.

He studied me though, locked his eyes with mine, and I didn't break the lock.

He then smiled. "Chandria, relax. I know you didn't do this. It's not in you. Plus, I saw the tape." He raised a brow. "Everything. Our cameras have a light on them even when the lights are out. I'll turn it over to the authorities."

I exhaled deeply.

And there is a possibility you can keep your job if—"

"If what, Ronald?" I was getting relieved by the second.

He bit his bottom lip. "I think you know. I want those juicy lips on me right now. Come here." He rubbed his crotch, threw his head back, and moaned, "You are so fucking hot. You look even better than Halle Berry and that other chick, Beyoncé."

I shook my head. "Wait! Wait! What are you saying? That after all of this, I need to sleep with you to keep working here?"

"Yes."

I stared at him and shook my head. "You saw me get raped on that tape! I won't. After what I had to go through, please don't put me in that corner. You don't know what I have been through in my life because of men who wanted to get their rocks off. I have suffered for years from it. The thought of sleeping with another man makes me sick. This job means something to me. It gives me purpose, hope that I can be something more than what I was. I'm setting an example for my son every day when I get up and go to work. I don't ever want to go back to the person I was before I got this job. Matter of fact, sir, don't pay me anything. I'll work my same hours and don't give me a check until I earn back all that money. Just please let me keep my job."

He was silent for a minute, like he was really considering what I had just said.

"This shouldn't be so hard. Do you think you are better than me?"

It was like he was shocked that I wouldn't leap over the table and sex him!

I didn't answer the question though. I wanted to keep this job, so I kept my mouth closed.

He stared at me for a moment before he said. "You black bitch, I'm sick of chasing you! Nigger, get the fuck out of my office!"

Chapter 27

Goldie

God, I can't believe I'm doing this, I thought to myself. My legs were tossed in the air, and Rick was going to town on my clit. He was eating my pussy so well.

I tossed my hands in my hair and screamed, "Damn! You are so fucking goooood to me!"

I opened my eyes to see his broad shoulders bent over as he moved his tongue in a half-circle on my clit while tossing fingers in my pussy. Rick had skills, yeah, but how was the dick?

When I felt myself creaming, and my legs shaking like I was going to pee on myself, he came up and flipped me on top of him. Then he slid his dick in a condom.

I rose a little and inched myself onto his dick, which was fat, and squatted, so I could get all of him, and sat down. His whole nine inches disappeared inside my pussy.

He groaned in his throat and lay his palms flat on my plump breasts. Then he rubbed his hands in a circular motion on my nipples.

I screamed and slid up and down faster, creating tightness in my belly and a bomb-ass sensation in my pussy. Then I shoved a titty in his mouth.

When I tightened my muscles on his, he gripped my hips and slammed me down repeatedly.

Then he rolled me over on my back, cocked both of my legs on his neck, and dove right back into my pussy.

He dipped his face closer to me for a kiss, but I turned my face away. He looked confused. To divert his attention from my rejection, I tightened my pussy muscles.

He took to kissing and sucking on my fingers. He bit down on my thumb and squeezed one of my butt cheeks with his other hand. "You wanna cum with me, Goldie? Huh?"

"Yesssssssss! Yes!"

He started pumping harder and rubbed his finger up and down my clit. "Cum for me, baby," he whispered in my ear. "Cum with me."

Too late. My pussy had already started squirting my juices well before he got his.

And he had the nerve to wanna cuddle afterward. Shit! I pulled away from his ass, slid out of the bed, and proceeded to put on my clothes.

His eyebrows burrowed together. "What's wrong, baby?"

I shook my head, offered a tight smile, and slipped on my shirt. "Nothing."

He watched me silently, his eyes saying, "You don't have to."

I threw him the peace sign and was out.

I went back to the beach and found a spot on the sand. I tried to wash the image of my mother out of my head. I kept seeing her face all of a sudden. I felt like I had betrayed her. I wiped away the tears pouring out of my eyes.

I froze when I heard feet behind me.

"If I came on too strong, I'm sorry."

I chuckled and stood to my feet and faced him. "Shit, me and my crew . . . I don't think you could ever come on too strong for us. This"—I spread my arms wide—"everything that you did, was all beautiful. I wouldn't have ever been able to experience something like this on my own. Hell, I don't even know where this place is on a map."

Why was I crying again?

He took a step toward me, but I placed a hand up, stopping him.

"Look, this is not one of those 'what do you want from me?' or 'with a girl like me?' because, you know what, I have none of those issues."

"Then what is it, Goldie?"

"Okay, fuck it! What do you want?"

Rick laughed. "Goldie, I don't want anything from you. Okay, fuck it! I do."

I laughed. "I'm an orphan, officer. You know where my mama is? In a ground decomposing, or probably, after all this time, decomposed completely. A cop shot her right in front of me and he got off. So all my life I've had this love-hate relationship with cops. I hate 'cause they killed my mama, all I ever had. I feel like every second that I spend with you, I'm spitting on her grave. And then I can't completely hate cops because my daddy was one." I paused. "And that's not the worst part. I have always felt like my mother's death was my fault. If I had just kept my ass in the car, she would still be here."

As I rehashed how it all went down to him, he simply nodded.

"I made it even worse, the way I carried on after she died, partying, messing around with men I had no business messing with, disrespecting my grandma. I drove her away. I carried on like my mama didn't teach me nothing, like her death didn't mean anything to me. But, really, her death changed my whole life. Since the age of fourteen, the way

I survived was being with older men. My first boyfriend was thirty-three, and I hadn't even started my period yet. In return for a roof over my head and food, all I ever had to do was sleep with him. All those years, that's how I ate, off men, with this." I gestured toward my body. "And I'm fucking tired of living this way. So tell me, mister officer, when we get home, are you gonna still want me, now that you got my goodies and all?"

Rick stepped closer and closer, until I found myself up in his arms.

He whispered in my ear, "Some time, affection, sex, some head here and there, movie dates, a couple of cooked meals."

Confused, I pulled away. "What?"

"That's what I want from you."

I giggled and buried my head in his chest.

I guess sometimes you never know.

Chapter 28

Cha

When it rains, man, it sure as heck pours. I thought on my way back from the county office. Ronald stated in my termination letter that I had misappropriated funds by illegally putting overtime on my pay stub, which I never did. I didn't want to battle with him, so I left it alone.

I thought I still had my county money, but I was in for a rude awakening there too. The county sent me a termination letter saying I made too much from my job and didn't report it. At first I didn't get it and thought it was some mistake. Then I realized it was the overtime! So when I called to find the balance on my EBT card I discovered that all I had was thirty dollars in food stamps and no cash aid. They had calculated all I had made that month and determined that I wasn't eligible for any money. I felt so stupid for forgetting to report that overtime he had put on my pay stub. I sat in that county office battling for my life and there was really nothing I could do. I had messed up royally and I knew that the county didn't care even if it was a simple mistake. Although they make mistakes all the time and it's like oh, well. What the hell was I going to do?

The lady looked at me like I was so beneath her. Maybe I was.

"You know what the guidelines are, Chandria. You're not a baby. It clearly states on your CA-7 that you are to report *any* extra income."

After cashing my check, I had returned the money right back to my supervisor. So technically there was no extra income. "But I did."

She rolled her eyes and shoved a paper my way. "On your pay stubs, it shows, for the month of November, you made an additional seven hundred dollars."

"But those are the pay stubs I turned in, ma'am."

"Right, but you didn't put in on your CA-7."

The County had so many technicalities for the pennies they were giving to struggling mothers.

"But don't you think that, if I was trying to hide the extra income, I wouldn't have turned in the pay stubs?"

She placed her hand in my face like I was a child. "You have two choices: You can go get a job and work like the rest of the world, since you don't like the way we do things, or you can wait thirty days and get back on the county." She smirked. "Something tells me you will pick the latter."

It was November fifteenth. I wasn't getting another check from my old job, and all the county gave me this month was thirty dollars in food stamps.

"But what am I supposed to do for this month and next month?"

"I just explained to you what you could do." She snatched up her files and left me sitting there, hopeless.

The Long Beach Transit bus let me off right in front of the Carmelitos.

I walked inside the complex and took a deep breath.

The good part about living in a low-income building was, if you had no income, you didn't have to pay rent. But the gas company, light company, and phone company and grocery stores didn't have the same policy.

"Hey, Cha."

I glanced up to see one of my married neighbors lushing me up and down. I put my head down and kept on walking past his lot. I had two more lots to go until I reached mine.

Another dude told the neighbor that had said hello to me, "Damn! She got a big ass!"

I ignored the comment and continued down until I made it to my lot.

Once I made it to my building, I was on my way to Tina's next door to collect Omari but stopped myself. I couldn't face him now. Everything was coming down on me hard. It's amazing how things can go from being soooo good to horrible. I didn't even want to wake up in the morning now, when prior to this, I loved it and was loving life. I hadn't felt that way since Onyx was alive.

As I made it up the steps to my apartment, I heard Tina call my name. I turned around and watched her make her way toward me.

Tina was a shapely, petite woman with skin the color of bronze and moles surrounding her eyes. She wasn't much older than me, but life had pretty much aged her. Man, she was a smart woman and had so many skills. She could sing and dance better than Ciara.

I would always ask her, "Why don't you go after it again?"

And she'd always say, "I'll leave those dreams for my kids. I'll just watch them go after theirs."

Tina gave me a smile I couldn't give back.

"Girl, this is a first. Since when do you not come and snatch up Omari?"

"Is he okay?"

"You gotta ask? You know he straight. He in there watching cartoons with the rest of the kids."

"Okay. Cool, girl."

"Man, we sure miss getting that Taco Bell."

I nodded miserably. This was the time I usually came back from work with bags of burritos, tacos, nachos, and some of those cinnamon twists. It had been officially two weeks since I had lost my job. I thought back to the day I had lost it. The stupid choice I made. Once I walked out of Taco Bell in tears I went to Dr. Baker for help.

That day, I remember walking down the street and thinking, *This shit don't make a bit of sense to me. It couldn't be what they all said about me when I was in that group home, that this was my fault.* Mr. Porter was jabbing me between my legs with his fingers, saying all the while, "You know what you were doing looking at me like that, girl." Then he would sniff his fingers and say, "Umm . . . smell good too." Then he would lick them.

At ten his sons holding me by my hair and shoving their penises in my mouth, their fingers wrapped around my neck and threatening to squeeze if I even thought about biting down. No matter what I did, I couldn't get that smell out of my hair. So I cut it all off.

Then on other occasions, Mr. Porter was shoving his penis up my butt, making me bleed for days after that. And I could only lie on my stomach or sit on the side of my butt cheeks. He'd told me, "You been asking for this."

Now years later I wanted to know what I had done to make this man I had trusted, Dr. Baker come on to me like that. I really trusted this doctor. Then he goes and pulls this. I mean, I was making such progress with him. The sessions gave me hope that I could heal and move on with my life, find love, and provide a good home for my baby, if I could just get this stuff out of my head.

And just as quickly as that hope came, it was going. But it wasn't completely gone.

I had to fix this. The doctor couldn't be like the others. Maybe he was drunk or smoked a little weed that night. I mean, doctors are human. Maybe he was a jokester or just testing me. Maybe, just maybe, I was reading too much into this stuff. I prayed to God that I was. I needed him, the optimism he gave me when I had sessions with him. Or maybe he was serious. He was, after all, a man. But he had to value his job. So if I checked him and let him know that I wasn't gonna tolerate flirting, he'd stop, apologize, and go back to keeping it professional.

Yeah, he would, I smiled. A woman has to demand respect, and if I check him one good time, he will know what the deal is. Then we could go back to my therapy.

Once I made it to Dr. Baker's office, I brushed past the secretary. He was sitting behind his desk when I stormed in.

"Why, Dr. Baker? Why did you have to say what you said to me?"

He looked up surprised. He waved his hand at his secretary, who was close on my heels, and she walked out. He got up and closed the door behind her.

"Have a seat, Chandria."

"No! I'm cool standing." I crossed my arms under my chest. "I mean, I respected you the utmost. I told you some personal stuff, and you—"

"I—"

"No!" I surprised myself with how sharp I came at him. "Listen, don't talk! I'm a grown woman, not some hood rat running 'round here. Now I'm going to let that mess you said over the phone pass, but if I'm going to continue to see you, you would need to control what comes out of your"—I felt a hand rub my ass.

That was it. Dude and Ronald's face flashed before me, and I lost it. I spun around and swung.

The next thing I know, he grabbed my arms and twisted them behind my back. I opened my mouth to scream, but he covered it with his hand. He was trying to kiss me.

I whimpered, praying it wouldn't happen to me again, as he pushed me back against his desk.

My fighting couldn't stop him, so when he freed one of his hands to grab one of my breasts, I snatched up a heavy paperweight from his desk and bashed his head with it. I pulled away and dropped the now bloody paperweight as he howled in pain. I then ran from his office, past the secretary, bawling all of the way.

Looking back on that day, I kept asking myself, *What would make me want to go back to a man who said what he'd said?* It's easy. When you become victimized for so long, you either believe it's your fault, or you hate yourself so much you want to believe it's your fault, 'cause you can't understand why God could be so cruel and keep subjecting you to pain. So if you feel it is you, you feel if you change yourself you can in some way change the situation.

See, with Dr. Baker, I was filled with so much hope. Then that was snatched away from me. Then I found a way to give myself that hope with the job. Then it was snatched away from me. Where was I gonna get it from now? That's why I went back to him. But it just made things worse.

***

"Cha? Cha, you with me, girl?"

I nodded. "Sorry, Tina. What were you saying?"

"Girl, you know for the past three months I been putting away all the childcare money you been giving me. I'm going to Big Lots to get some of them sales on Christmas toys for my kids. You wanna come? If you do, you gotta be up around four thirty."

Just then my phone rang. I ignored it.

Dang! Christmas just came out of nowhere like it did every year. And I had no extra dough for Omari's Christmas stuff. I bit my bottom lip.

The phone rang again. It would be off soon.

"I'll let you know, Tina. Tell Omari I will get him soon." I dashed in the house, but didn't make it in time to answer the phone.

I wondered if Goldie had called, so I sat on my couch with the phone in hand and dialed her number. She didn't answer. Where was she? It wasn't like her to not return her calls. I hadn't heard from her in over a week. I knew she was kicking it tough with that officer, but still.

But, then again, if I was Goldie, would I wanna hear negativity from a person all of the time? Maybe not.

I sighed, and called the last person I wanted to call. Red.

Chapter 29

Red

I snickered as I watched Cha out of the corner of my eye as she sat with her legs open on the bed. She didn't have a clue what was about to go down tonight. Within a few minutes her ass would be straight amped.

She was loaded off a double dose of Spanish fly that was ground in the margaritas I made. And that ain't all. The dumb bitch took a hit off my blunt that didn't have just weed, but cocaine too. She had never hit weed before, so she didn't know the difference.

I wasn't no addict, but I did indulge every now and then. I was going to have some muthafucking fun and get paid for it.

I leaned down on my knees and deep-throated Don, both of us high on ecstasy. I moaned and said, "Ouu, baby, your dick is so big." I licked up and down his shaft, and he started groaning and saying all kinds of shit.

Cha started breathing harder as she watched us. She didn't know what the fuck was wrong with her. She came and stood behind Don and started rubbing his shoulders, like I told her she had to do earlier. Just an hour earlier, Cha had popped up at my crib looking so distressed, I thought the bitch was going to take her own life. Since I was handling business with Don, I almost told her ass to kick rocks, but while I was in the bathroom, he invited her in. I told her to wait in my room while I conducted my business.

Initially, when I met Don, it was her that he wanted to talk to, but I put my game on his ass and he ain't said nothing 'bout her since.

"So what's up? Why you on me so tough, girl?" he asked me.

To tell the truth, I wasn't on his mongrel-looking ass so tough. I was on the contact he could hook me up with. Rock, the nigga he worked for.

Don did pretty good for himself as a drug dealer, but I had no desire to be a drug dealer's girl. Shit! You really get no spoils, if you ask me. I wanted my own shit, my own dope, my own money, not to be with an ugly-ass man who had a bitch like me in every city, and when he felt like it, would kick me down with a couple hundred. And I knew Don worked the muscle for Rock, so I basically wanted to be put on and would do whatever I needed to do to be put on.

"You gotta hook me up with your boy Rock. I want in on those transports, Don. A bitch is hungry and hardworking."

"That's why you invited me over here?"

"It ain't the only reason," I lied. *Dear God, I hope I don't have to fuck this ugly-ass man to get what I want. I would have to really dope myself up.*

"Why should I put you on when I can put on any bitch in these Carmelitos?"

"Because they can't do what I can do. You know you can trust me."

"That's not what I mean, Red. Me calling Rock and putting you on is doing you a favor." He rubbed on his crotch. "I don't just do muthafuckas favors."

"Well, what you want to persuade you? Some pussy? Your dick sucked? If you'd just said that, we wouldn't be having this conversation."

What? My head snapped back.

"Niggas don't want what they can have. They want what they can't have." He jerked his head toward the room Cha was in.

The shit enraged me, but still, business is business. "What the fuck you saying?"

"You hook it up to it's all three of us, I'll talk to Rock, and you'll be moving weight."

"You serious?"

He nodded.

I went in the kitchen and poured Cha a drink. Then I went into the room and handed it to her. I let her take a few sips.

"So what up, girl?"

She shook her head. "A lot, Red, but I don't want to get into it. I came over here 'cause I need your help."

"What you need?"

"A loan." She downed the margarita like it was water.

"Fuck a loan! I got a real way for us to make some money."

"Humph. What?"

I pointed to the living room and whispered, "He wants a threesome with the both of us."

She laughed. "Girl, are you serious?"

"Yeah, bitch. Wouldn't have said it if I wasn't."

"Red, I can't do that, you know."

"I know you want Omari to have some shit under the tree is what I know," I said dryly. "I know you want a fucking tree! Look, I ain't got time to convince you. Either you want it, or you don't, but you ain't gotta do shit. He is willing to pay us well, girl. Well. And you ain't gotta do nothing. Just lay there naked and let him lush on you. I'm the one that's gonna be fucking him. All you gotta do is sit there, show your pussy. Shit! That's all. He'll pay you four hundred too. Just sit there naked and rub his back while I do all the damn work." And since I knew she worshipped Goldie's raggedy ass, I lied, saying, "Goldie did it with me before."

Cha looked surprised. "She did?"

"It ain't something you just go around telling people, girl," I said quickly. I figured she was wondering why Goldie hadn't told her. "It's all about fulfilling a fantasy. He's an ugly-ass nigga with a lot of money. He'd never get girls like us if he was broke. Girl, it's nothing. And, in the meantime, you can put away a chunk of dough."

And here we are.

"Thanks, baby," Don told Cha. He reached up and grabbed her round coconut titties and squeezed them luscious nipples, and she started moaning like crazy.

Damn! Ecstasy never made me feel like this. And I downed them like Skittles.

Cha didn't indulge in any of this shit and the only reason she did today was to loosen up to do this. All I told her she had to do was sit buck-ass naked. *Ha!*

"Come closer, Cha," I said.

When she did, crouching closer to him so he could give her the tongue kiss, I stuck one of my fingers up her pussy, and she moaned, rocking against it. I could tell my girl ain't had none in a while.

Meanwhile, Don was going crazy, stroking his shit. "You going to get down with her, babe?" he asked me.

I nodded. "Lay down, Cha."

"Okay, Onyx."

What? My girl was hallucinating for sure, and her eyes were wild as hell.

I crouched between her legs and started sucking her pussy. Man, was it pretty.

Cha was thrashing her head from side to side, calling me her baby daddy name, saying that she loved him and missed him and that she was happy he came back to her.

She held my head between her legs, and as I suckled on her clit, she started convulsing.

Don took that as his cue to come behind me and shove his dick in my pussy.

"Awww shit!" I moaned as he pumped into me. I started licking on that pussy savagely, probing it with my fingers.

Don plunged deeper into me then he pulled out. He rushed over to Cha and sprayed her chest and stomach with his dick then he yanked her by her neck and forced her to lick off the remaining cum. Then he flipped her over like she was a rag doll.

"Nigga, what the fuck you doing?" I demanded.

"Getting what I want."

Don stuck a few fingers in her asshole, spat in it, and inserted his dick in her virgin ass like it was my pussy.

I laughed.

My guess was, the pain of getting ass-fucked, I'm sure for the first time, had Cha screaming. Or the drugs were wearing off.

"Get off of me!" she screamed over and over again.

Don backed up disappointed, and Cha slid off the floor to her feet. She looked at me like I betrayed her. Then she looked at Don and down her naked body

"Where are my clothes?"

I pointed at the floor.

She yanked them on and in a flash was out the door.

Chapter 30

Goldie

Something was up with Cha. I had been calling and calling her, and she wouldn't answer her phone. Since I was back in town me, her, and Red were supposed to meet up for drinks. I'd even offered to pay her neighbor to watch Omari, but she never showed up. It ended up being just me and Red. And for some reason, Red was tight lipped about Cha's no show. So I took matters into my own hands.

The next day, I paused outside her apartment. I peeked in the window and saw Omari in the living room on the couch. I could hear the TV on, so I assumed he was watching it.

I tapped on the window. His head popped up, and he immediately ran to the window and slid it open.

"Hey, boo," I said.

He gave me a snaga tooth smile, with his handsome butt.

"Hi, auntie."

"Open up and let me in. I got you some breakfast." I walked back around to the door and waited for him to unlock it. "Hey, baby boy." I held the bags in one hand and gave him a hug.

He grinned and threw his little arms around me.

"Here." I handed him a bag of food and stepped aside. "The pancakes and sausages are for you. The croissant is for your mom." I looked around the living room. "Where is she?"

"In bed. She don't feel good."

"She don't feel good?" I twisted my lips to one side.

Omari sat down at the table and sat the bag down. I reached in the bag and handed him his pancakes and juice. Then I opened the syrup and poured it on his pancakes, and he began slicing them.

"I'll go take this to your mom." I walked toward the hallway thinking, *Damn! Something is wrong with my friend!*

I found her lying in bed not 'sleep, but staring at the ceiling, like something was really up there.

"Girl, you act like there's a flat-screen up there."

She didn't laugh or even offer a smile.

I sat next to her on the bed she shared with Omari. "I bought you some food."

"I'm not hungry."

She turned away. Sadness didn't take away how pretty that girl was. Even early in the morning.

"What's wrong, Cha?"

She ignored me.

"Cha!"

I narrowed my eyes when she didn't respond. Then I leaped on top of her and started tickling her underneath her arms, thinking she was going to laugh, or at least bust a smile.

She yelled out," Stop, Goldie! Damn!"

I moved away quickly. "What the fuck is wrong with you?"

She sat up in the bed.

"What?"

She raised her knees to her chest, and buried her face

in them. I couldn't see her face, but when I saw her shoulders shaking, I knew she was crying.

"Cha, I'm really worried now. Girl, what is it?"

She stretched her legs back out and wiped her face free of tears. "Red, said it wasn't going to be a big deal. She said y'all did it before and—"

"Whoa! Stop! Red said me and her did what?"

"She said you and her did a three-way together before with a dude."

I stood with my hands on my hips. "No, the fuck. I have not ever done that shit! I don't ever need muthafucking dough that bad." I sat back down.

She went back to sobbing.

"You and Red did that?"

She squeezed her eyelids tight and nodded her head. "With Don."

Don worked for a big-time drug dealer. I'm talking big-time. One night at a hood party he'd made it a point one night to let Cha know he was feeling her, but Cha wasn't going for it. So, of course, Red saw dollar signs and pushed up on him.

"Cha, what exactly happened?"

"I needed the money. Goldie, I still do need a whole lot. They cut my county check this month and my food stamps."

"Why?"

"I don't know. It's got something to do with that job and overtime. I lost that job." She started shaking like she was revisiting something against her will. "But I don't wanna talk about that. See, Red made it seem like it was nothing, that all I was going to have to do was sit naked and rub his back. That's it. But it ended up being a whole lot more. I don't know what came over me, but I was so drunk, I ended up sleeping with him." She took a deep breath.

"She knows how I feel about that. That I have no desire to be with anyone since Onyx died. And I still haven't dealt with that. Now I'm trying to, and seeing this damn doctor, and he tries to rape me."

I shook my head. "What? Did I miss all of this while I was away?"

Instantly I felt regretful. Cha needed me, and I wasn't there for her. And she had nobody else. Red knew that shit and took advantage of the situation.

"I can't do this anymore."

"Can't do what anymore, Cha?"

"Life."

That made my heart pound, made me want to cry, hearing her say something like that. My eyes started to water. I blinked rapidly in hopes they would dry up.

"How much did Red promise you for the three-way?"

"Four hundred. I needed to pay bills, and Christmas is right around the corner."

"What did you get?"

"Nothing."

I wanted to nut up when she said that shit. "You know what? That was dirty. She played you."

"Yeah. I can't explain it, Goldie. I know I don't drink too much, so maybe that's why that shit I downed fucked with me so bad. I was out of it, doing some shit . . ." Her voice trailed off.

I knew she wasn't telling me everything.

"I got blowed."

I fell back on the bed and started laughing. "You smoked some weed, girl?"

She nodded. "That mess had me tripping . . . down for whatever."

That's when my smile dropped. Red wouldn't! I shook my head, hoping Red didn't put some shit in Cha's weed just to fuck with her. Red couldn't be that fucked up. Cha would have never suspected it. She was so naïve. I sighed.

"To tell the truth, I did it not just to be able to do that shit, but to get my mind off what that damn doctor did and all the other stuff. The job, I know it was rinky-dink, but it made me finally feel like I had a reason to hold my head high. When I went into the stores and bought stuff, it was money I earned. My spirit was coming back." She smiled when she said that. "That doctor was giving me so much hope that I could be right. Goldie, I ain't never felt like I could be right."

"But why do you think that shit? Cha, you the kindest person I have ever known, and I know it's fucked up all the stuff that has happened to you."

"I ain't right, Goldie. I'm all screwed up, girl. Ruined."

I didn't say anything else. She wouldn't have believed me if I'd pointed out all the things about her that were so beautiful and pure.

To be real, if I were her, I wouldn't have believed it coming from my friend either. Who can go through what she did and come out feeling fucking normal? It's a wonder she even got up in the morning. She was a great mom, the best I have ever seen. All that love and patience she shows Omari.

The only place she ever learned love from was from Onyx, never from a parent. Even I had some to hold onto from my mama. But Red's ass, I don't know what the hell she had. The bitch never talked about where she came from. All I knew was that her mom died when she was damn near grown, and that she hustled from that point on.

"Has she even called you?"

Cha shook her head.

"The bitch could have had the decency to have at least given you the money. She knows damn well you need it. I'm going to see what I could do to help you out this month on your bills and food."

"You got extra dough like that, Goldie?"

The only money I had coming in was my financial aid check for my books and tuition. But that shit wasn't here. The one thing I learned in my life was not to count on money that wasn't in your hand or reach. Publishers Clearing House still ain't came to my crib with my million-dollar check, despite how many magazines I done ordered from they ass.

"I got you, girl," I said, lying through my teeth. "Don't even trip."

"Thanks, Goldie. I hope it won't mess you up."

"Girl, it's cool. Anyway, you know I'm enrolled in college. I'm supposed to start in a few weeks."

"I didn't know you checked in. Wow!" Cha's eyes got bright, and she smiled a proud smile, like in that moment she was looking up to me.

I dropped my eyes. "To tell the truth, nobody knew. I don't know, Cha. I didn't really tell anybody and get their hopes up and my punk-ass don't end up going."

"You'll go."

She smiled at me again. It was so sweet, it had to make you wonder why would anyone want to take advantage of her, especially someone that's supposed to be her girl.

"Yeah? Well, school starts next month. Let's see if I'm gonna go, or make this another hustle, getting financial aid."

"You gonna go. You smart. Remember when we took those GED exams and you passed on the first try, and I failed?"

I slapped her arm. "Heiffa, you never showed up. That's why you failed."

She laughed.

"But, you and Omari, you guys are going to be just fine. And, Red, yeah, she our girl and all, but the bitch can be foul. I'll be sure to curse her out." I leaned over and hugged her, whispering, "You gonna be fine, girl."

Chapter 31

Red

Cha was cool and shit, but it was always "money over friends." Fuck the bullshit. Hoes were always last on my list of priorities. I didn't give a damn if she did have a kid. She lay down and had that fucking pig. I wasn't gonna sit nowhere and pity anybody. I could use that time being more proactive. That night I realized niggas will pay up for a fantasy. Eating Cha's pussy wasn't a bad thing either. But I know her trick ass probably went crying to Goldie, who probably didn't give a damn because she was too busy fucking that cop.

I wanted to prove my assumption for sure, so I rolled over to Goldie's lot and parked. I saw her car parked, so I knew she was home, unless she was with Rick.

Before I could get out my car, she came out wearing a robe and was carrying a plate in her hand. *Since when did the bitch own a robe?*

Before she made it past the grass, a squad car with Rick in it pulled up and stopped. She walked up to his car and handed him the plate.

What is this shit?

Then she leaned in the car and kissed Rick, who leaned a hand out the car and smacked her on the ass. All she probably was to him was project pussy.

Once he drove away, she turned and headed toward the mailboxes. That's when I snuck out of my car and crept up on her.

"Boo, bitch!" I shouted.

She dropped her mail and stood in a fighting stance. The mail fell a few inches from my feet. I leaned over and plucked it off the ground, allowed my eyes to scan it before handing it back to her. And my greedy eyes weren't deceiving me. It was a check.

"Long Beach City College?"

She snatched it back from me and rolled her eyes.

"What the fuck you getting mail from them for?"

"Why I can't?"

I smiled, understanding her attitude. Cha had dropped a dime on me. Sentimental bitch.

"Aye, you know that was some foul shit that you did."

I spread my arms wide. "What I do?"

She crossed her arms under her chest. "You know what she been through. She been abused, molested, raped, and shit. You know she is sensitive about men. Why you didn't just loan her the money? Why you involve her in that nasty shit?"

"Man, go on with that little princess bullshit. Cha grown, and she know how to ride dick like anybody else. If she having bad feelings about the choice she *made*, she can run to that damn counselor."

"He tried to rape her, Red!"

"What? Damn! I wish she would have told me."

"I know," Goldie said, temporarily forgetting she was pissed at me. "I wanna fuck him up too."

"Naw! Fuck that! We could have him come over and pretend we wanna fuck with him and rob his ass."

She shook her head at me. "You truly ain't shit."

I shrugged. I didn't give a fuck what anybody thought about me.

"I got something for that nigga, not like you give a fuck. I wonder what was really your motivation. To make money or to humiliate Cha? 'Cause if he could, he would have made Cha his woman." She locked eyes with me.

Damn! Cha talk too much. I waved my hand at her. "Fuck all of that. Let's go hang."

"Naw. I'm gonna find somebody to handle that punk-ass doc."

"I'm wit' it."

She frowned at me. "What you gonna do?"

"What you got in mind?"

"I was thinking about ruining his career, maybe getting him on tape with an underage girl, or just plain out having somebody fuck him up."

"Naw. I got an even better idea, girl. Don't even trip. I'm going to avenge Cha. You got any info on him?"

"Yes. I snatched this off her dresser." She pulled a card out of her bra and handed it to me.

"You just go brush your yellow-ass teeth."

"Fuck you, Red!" She walked off.

Ten minutes later, I found myself on the ho stroll. See, thing is, you'd be lucky to find a grown woman there, since most of the hoes were all underage. But I found what I was looking for.

Caramel was a fine-as-hell dick-slayer. The bitch was deadly.

I honked, and her big-booty self walked up to my ride and put her head in my window.

"What's up, Red?"

I didn't say shit. I just handed her the dude's business card.

"He kinda cute."

I passed her two twenties, gave her the peace sign, and drove away. I had one more thing to take care of.

Chapter 32

Goldie

The check was for two thousand dollars. Just to go to school? Man, this was the ultimate hustle.

I went through my schedule. The books for my four classes would be $250, and my tuition was already paid. That left me almost eighteen hundred dollars.

I was gonna break Cha off a cool five hundred to pay her bills, get some food, and a couple gifts for Omari for Christmas. I would throw the rest in the bank . . . well, after I opened up an account, which I still didn't have. One thing I knew was that I had no intentions of wasting this money so that meant no materialistic stuff for me.

"So what are your plans today?" Rick asked. He had called me on his break.

"Well, I'm getting ready to hit the bank. Then I'm going to visit my friend. Why you asking? You plan on sweeping me off my feet and taking me somewhere?"

"As a matter of fact, baby, yeah."

Ouuu, this man! "That's cool with me," I said, relaxing on my couch.

"What would you like? Dinner, movies, dancing? Wherever you wanna go."

"Dancing would be cool."

"Have you ever done salsa dancing?"

"I'm from the hood. Hello?"

"Have you?"

"No. You?"

"Yes."

"You such a square." I laughed.

Just then, my line beeped. "Hold on, Rick." I clicked over to discover it was Red.

"What you doing?" she asked.

"Why? Damn! I'm on the phone with my baby."

"You in the house for the night?"

"I'm going to visit Cha in a little while."

"Oh, okay. Hey, Goldie, can you ask your cop dude if he could drop by? I see some dude creeping by my steps."

"Yeah. Hold on, dumb ass." I clicked over. "Baby."

"Huh?"

"Do me a favor. My dumb-ass friend Red said there is some dude creeping by her pad."

"What lot does she live in?"

"The one you came to when you sexually harassed me that day the repo guy called you."

He chuckled. "Okay, baby."

"Thanks," I said sweetly. I clicked back over to Red. "He's on the way. Did you take care of the doctor?"

Red laughed. "Hell, yeah."

"Well, did he get arrested? Or, knowing you, did you get Blue to kick his ass?"

"Kick his ass? Arrested? Girl, I did something better. I paid a ho to push up on him and fuck him."

"What? That ain't doing shit. You did him a favor."

"No. The fuck, I didn't! Caramel, the ho I got, has full blown AIDS."

Chapter 33

Red

I sprayed some perfume on and walked up to the door when I heard my bell ring.

Rick's eyes must have damn near popped out of his head when he saw me standing there, ass buck-naked. I didn't have on shit, but a toe ring.

I gave him a half-smile along with a wink. "What it do, shorty?"

"Goldie said you called me over here for an emergency, not to see you naked."

"Naked? You ain't quite seen me naked yet." I crouched down so I was sitting on my floor in front of him. Then I opened my legs wide and used my fingers to open up the lips on my pussy. "Now you seeing me naked, officer."

He closed his eyes, shook his head, and said calmly, "I know how this works. You been her friend for a long time, I'm the new boyfriend in her life. So if I tell her, or before I even get to, you will tell her I pushed up on you, while I'm not going to say anything because I don't want to lose Goldie."

"Oh, yeah? And what the fuck is so special about Goldie's black ass, when you can hit this?"

He cleared his throat and looked above my head again. "She is everything you're not."

My mouth popped open at that comment. *Faggot!*

"I will check the perimeter then I'm leaving, ma'am."

"Fuck you!"

"Naw. I'm straight." He turned on his heels, mumbling, "My baby needs to get some new friends."

Chapter 34

Goldie

I couldn't even think straight. I felt so incredibly guilty about the shit Red did. I downed half a bottle of Patrón and passed out on the couch. The only reason I got my ass up and pulled myself together was because I had to go cash my check so I could take some of the money I had got from school to Cha.

I grabbed my keys and purse, and as soon as I stepped outside, locked my door, and turned around, somebody pressed a Glock deep in my face. His face was covered by a blue du-rag.

"Don't look at me, bitch!"

I closed my eyes briefly as he snatched my purse off my shoulders.

"Is it here?" he demanded.

"Is what here?"

He punched the side of my face. "What the fuck you mean, *what*, bitch?" He reached into my bun and yanked it out—my check, buried underneath in the swirl of my bun and stuck with a clip.

How the fuck did he know that?

With that, he bashed me in the mouth with his gun, knocking me clean and clear out.

Chapter 35

Cha

I was at the bottom of the barrel. All I had left in my house was a teaspoon of margarine and a bag of flour. Nothing else, no rice, potatoes, nothing.

"I can't do it this time, Cha. I'm sorry."

I smiled and nodded at my neighbor. She had been feeding Omari for the past three days. She had kids of her own. What was I going to do?

Chapter 36

Red

Ain't that I needed the money. I just didn't want Goldie to have it. *Does that make me a bitch? Maybe. Shit, at least I'm admitting it.* There are just things you don't confide in other people. Like where you hide your dough.

Once I made it inside Blue's crib, he tossed the check my way.

I tossed it back. "I don't want that shit!" I sat down. "That ain't what I came here for. I came to see if you was telling the truth about 'ole girl."

"That's fucked up that you did your girl like that."

I ignored him and focused on the scene in front of me. My former neighbor, presently a dope fiend, "Strawberry," was sucking dick right in front of me. It was Blue's broke ass homie, Seku to be exact. Her big ol' booty was jiggling like crazy as she licked up and down his shaft.

She was so stupid. Neither of them slang crack!

I threw my head back and laughed when Seku took his Cisco bottle and emptied it all over her matted-ass hair. I guess losing her three kids was too much for her to bear. I say, fuck them little pigs. I wonder what the courts would think of her if they saw her now. Like Forrest Gump said, "Stupid is as stupid does."

I laughed as Seku yanked his dick out of her mouth. "Move, bitch! You can't suck a dick, no way." He shoved it back in his pants.

But no dope did she get. She had exhausted her options to get the rock her eyes desperately craved. I knew ol' girl was fien'in'.

"What you looking at Red for?" Blue said. "She ain't got no dick."

"Yeah. But my kitty need to get licked, just like your shit do, nigga." I looked at her. "You wit' it, boo? You wanna lick on me for some high?"

She dropped her eyes as hatred for me filled them. Then the hate dropped from her eyes, and she slowly nodded.

Seku laughed. "Aye! I can't believe you doing that shit, Red!"

I ignored him and slid my mini skirt all the way up to my waist. I wasn't wearing no panties. I then let ol' girl slip between them. I bobbed her head in my hands as she took her tongue and probed my insides. I tossed my head back and moaned, "Aww shit! Right there! Lick my pearl tongue, bitch."

I controlled her better than them niggas did. I had no shame in my game. If they could sit in front of me and get their dick sucked, why the fuck couldn't I sit in front of them and get my pearl tongue licked?

But I didn't let the bitch make me cum. Instead, I squeezed my muscles together, gripping her head, and managed to get a squirt of piss into her mouth. "Move, bitch!" I kicked her out of my way and pulled my skirt back down.

Then I threw them the peace sign and was out. I was on my way to Don's crib. They had offered me a last minute assignment that my ass couldn't turn down.

So far, the shit I had done was simple. I got hired at LaX. The manager there was also in on it. Don provided me with a fake ID and social security card. My job, which was my cover, was scanning baggage through the screener. Whenever Rock sent a person in I was notified and I let their luggage pass through. The shit was so fucking cool. While Rock was like the fucking invisible man raking in most of the dough, he did check me before I started my first day.

After they handed me my ID and social security card I thought I was sailing free, but Don burst that bubble when he handed me a cell phone.

"Rock wanna speak to you."

I snatched the phone and said, "What it do, Rock?" like I knew him.

"Listen, project bitch."

Bitch?

"I don't give a damn if the head of the DEA is chasing you down on TV with helicopters above your head, if some gun-toting crack head rob you, or if your brother smoke my shit by accident. What's gone is gone, and it ain't coming back, regardless of the reason. I have a strong rep on these streets, so if you, ever take my shit, Red, I will have you killed."

That made my heart skip a beat. I almost dropped the phone, but I tried to keep my game face on. "Why you gotta come at me like that?"

The line went dead.

But I always followed proper protocol. Which is why I was surprised that they were loading the trunk of my car with something other than sticky-icky.

"What the fuck is that?" I asked Don.

"The fuck you think it is, Red?"

"I ain't signed on to roll around with powder in my car."

"Red, all the fuck you doing is dropping the shit off."

"But it's cocaine!"

"Look, you wanna make this money or not? 'Cause I'm sure I can find some ho around here to do the shit for way cheaper than your ass."

"I got you, Don. Damn! I just don't wanna get caught up in no shit."

"You punkin' the game with the scary shit. Either you gonna go, or you ain't! And, trust, if you drive yo' high-yellow ass away, I'm letting Rock know, and you off the line."

I remained silent.

"Red, you live in Long Beach. LA ain't but twenty minutes away."

I wanted to ask, "Then why don't you do the shit?" I sure as hell didn't want to do this shit. I knew Fig was always a hot-as-fuck street with the cops.

"How many drop-offs am I doing?" I asked. Before, I would take just one trip, and it ain't never been this much dope.

"Just one. The dope spot on Fig. That's my main house where they cook the shit. Then it's going to be dispersed to the other dope spots, Compton, San Pedro, Wilmington, Long Beach, and Lynwood. You said you wanted to be on, Red."

I stared him down and gritted my teeth, itching to dump that shit out of my car.

Then I turned on my ignition. "I ain't punking shit! Close the trunk!" But it turned out that I only managed to drive up the block to a vacant parking lot. I sat in my car for a good ten minutes, scared to get my ass on that freeway. I tried to think: I could be done with that shit and be straight for a minute, maybe, not do anymore for Rock. Stack my cheese and move on. But on to what?

I wasn't fucking with Harem anymore. I had no other

options, but to deal with this. Stack enough to start my own dope house.

I tapped my fingers on the steering wheel, willing myself to start my car and pull out of my parking stall and get my ass on the freeway. I kept telling myself this would set me up with my own dope spot, find a house or even an apartment, get a few workers, and I'll be straight, but, damn, I couldn't bring myself to start that car.

Just then my phone rang. At first I was going to ignore it, but I saw it was Cha. Guess the Orphan Annie bitch wasn't mad at me no more. I snatched it open. "What it do, shorty?"

Chapter 37

Cha

"Hey, Red," I said, desperate. "You heard from Goldie? She was supposed to drop off some dough for me."

"Maybe she went out of town with her cop dude."

"Okay."

I had to get some cash fast. I was a minute away from selling my behind. No lights or phone would do that to you. Not to mention an empty stomach and a vacant look in my son's eyes.

"I'm hungry, Mommy."

"I know, baby." I pulled him on my lap and rubbed his little tummy. "Red, could I get that money you promised me?"

"Girl, my bad about that situation with the doc. Yeah, you can have it, but I need a favor. I'll add another hundred to the four. It don't involve a threesome, though."

I sighed. "What kind of favor?"

She couldn't just give me what she promised. Red was a renege kind of person, so I accepted that. Wasn't no point in trying to change her now. I had exhausted all my resources, and Omari needed to be fed.

I also needed to hurry up on my neighbor's phone. "What is it, Red?

"These dudes going to look at my car for me. Something is wrong with it. I think I need another timing belt or some shit like that. But, girl, I'm having some serious cramps and I just threw up, so if you could just drive my car to the mechanic, I would appreciate it, Cha."

"To where?"

"To LA."

"Just to drive your car to LA?" *Why was she being so nice?*

"Don't I owe you some money anyway? The extra hundred is 'cause you my girl. I mean, if you don't want the shit . . . and there's an extra ten for my little nigga."

"You don't even like Omari."

"I'm tapping into my maternal instincts."

Red was really growing up, or maybe she felt like dirt for that three-way mess.

"Heaven forbid," I said, joking.

"What the fuck you mean by that?"

"Girl, calm down. We joking, right?"

I heard her snort.

"What time do I need to be there?" I asked quickly, before she changed her mind.

"Within the next thirty, to make this money."

Chapter 38

Goldie

Funny how people you lived by all your life don't give ten tears in a bucket about your ass. Case in point, it was the officer who found me lying on my steps with my muthafucking mouth busted. My blurry eyes saw the officer with flowers. He instantly dropped to his knees and grabbed my face, along my neck, I guess, checking my pulse. I was conscious, but I felt myself going in and then right back out from the blow.

Today I was more than conscious, so I knew that was him sitting across from me. He even cracked a smile at me. I couldn't return it. That would have hurt my mouth.

I threw up the peace sign, and he laughed. I know I damn well looked a hot ghetto mess.

"Hey," I said softly.

"Hey. How do you feel?"

"Like shit."

"Did you get a look at the person who did this?"

"Don't trip," I managed. It was hard as hell to talk with my head still ringing.

"What, baby?"

"I think I know who did it." There was only one other person who knew where I stashed my dough.

"You do?" He had a surprised look on his face.

"Yeah."

"Okay, well, give me their names and descriptions." Rick pulled out a small notepad and a pen. "I'll put an APB on them right now."

I waved my hands at him like I was swatting flies away. "I'm not gonna turn them in."

"Why?"

"I'm not a snitch. I'll handle this shit on my own. I don't play that role."

He paused and stared at me hard. "So you mean to tell me that you know who robbed you and assaulted you and because you consider it snitching you're not going to let me know because I'm a cop?"

I nodded.

"Then, baby, I'm sorry to say, but that's bullshit."

I winced. He'd never spoke to me like that.

"Listen to me, You don't owe these streets shit! These streets don't got no loyalty, nor do they care about you Goldie. You need to get that shit through your head before you—"

"Before what?"

"Before these very same streets you care about so much kill you. Make you lose someone who loves you." He rubbed the front of his face with the palm of his hands. "Listen, baby, I took this job to protect people, not abuse or misuse them. I have not and don't plan on misusing you either. Now, will you tell me who did this to you?"

I turned my head to the side and lay on my pillow, so I didn't have to look in his eyes. I closed my eyes and still felt his presence standing over me. He stared at me for a long time, he had angry, disappointed eyes on me. I could feel them.

When I opened my eyes again, he was gone.

Chapter 39

Cha

I prayed on this, asked God to give me the answer. God I know you are not exactly proud of the direction your girl went down. I'm not either. But God Omari means everything to me and all I want, all I ever wanted was to make sure he is safe and well taken care of. I don't want him to go through any of what I had to. But I owe you and him more than this so I'm really gonna try get it together." I opened up my eyes and glanced at Omari sitting alongside me on his knees head bowed, hands clasped together.

"Amen," I said.

"Amen," he echoed.

"Omari, tomorrow mommy is going to look for another job, even if it kills me and even if I have to tug your behind with me."

He nodded. "Then can we get the Wii?"

"Omari!"

He clasped his hands over his mouth, stifling his giggle.

"I don't know about that no time soon. But what I do know is, mommy is going to step it up some more."

He nodded.

We had to hurry over to Red's house, so I could make

this money and get my utilities on. I figured me getting cut off the county was a blessing in disguise, since it gave me the push I needed to get myself together and go back out to the work force.

And, in the meantime, before finding a job, I could at least get the lights and phone back on, in case jobs would be calling, and even put some food in the house. Red was a blessing in disguise.

I slid on a pair of jeans while Omari watched and started to giggle. I glanced at him over my shoulder. "What you laughing at now, boy?"

"Your booty is so big, Mommy."

Embarrassed I covered my butt cheeks, laughing. "Where did that come from?"

"Malik told me that his daddy said that he wanted to hit it."

My eyes bucked.

"I told Malik that if his daddy hit my mama I was going to beat him up." Omari balled his little fists. "I promised daddy before he died I would protect my mama."

"Awww." I leaned down and hugged his little chest to mine. "You protect me just fine, baby. I love you so much."

"I love you too, Mommy, even though I'm not supposed to say that."

My eyes watered. I felt like I was going to cry, but the tears were good. I was gonna get it together.

"Okay." I released him and grabbed his jacket. I held it out for his little arms to slip into. I then zipped it up and said, "Let's go."

For a split second I was going to call Goldie before I headed out the door, but I figured she wouldn't answer. I smiled, happy she was happy, but really missing her guidance.

We walked out of my place headed to Red's spot.

Omari talked my ears off the whole way. "Mommy, where is Auntie Goldie?"

"I don't know. Come on, baby, it's getting late."

When we made it to Red's lot we found her sitting out on her porch when we approached her.

"Hey, girl!" she said. She handed me a piece of torn paper. "Take it to the address on here. It's on Fig." She handed me two hundred dollars. "You'll get the rest when you bring my car back home, girl."

I chuckled and shook my head at her. "She don't trust us, Omari."

Omari kept his eyes on his sneakers.

My eyes scanned the paper.

"It's off of 120, a brown-looking house."

That sounded easy.

"It shouldn't take too long for him to finish the shit. To tell you the truth, Cha, I owe you this money, so I appreciate you looking out for your girl. I owe you this for the three-way. Goldie told me you were upset behind that. I'm sorry, girl."

"Red."

"Naw, you don't have to explain. I should have given you what I promised you."

Now I felt bad for discussing Red with Goldie. It was my choice to smoke that crazy-ass weed. I wouldn't do it again. That's for sure. Red wasn't that bad.

I smiled. "You know I can drive the mess out of a freeway. Shouldn't take me no time, maybe fifteen minutes at best."

Red tossed me the keys.

"Bye, Red." Omari waved a hand at her.

"Bye, little nigga." She tossed a ten-dollar bill his way.

Chapter 40

Goldie

The hospital released me. My shit was still in pain, and I could only consume fucking liquids. Someway my cell phone was gone, and that's when I started piecing together what happened. I realized I didn't get a chance to give Cha any money. *Damn!* I hoped she had found a way. I also hoped it wasn't dealing with Red. I was going to personally take it upon myself to find out what I needed to know.

Once I made it to my house, I went inside and went straight to my room. I grabbed one of my shoeboxes under my bed, where I kept my 9 mm. I unlocked my safety, cocked the shit, locked it again and slipped it into the back pocket of my jeans.

I dug into my stash that was always only for emergencies. I pulled a hundred-dollar bill and two twenties.

I walked out my door and down the block and found Slow huddled in a corner, lighting his pipe. I gave him a few seconds to inhale that shit.

"Where Blue?"

He looked at me surprised, his eyes widened. Then he shrugged his shoulders.

"Don't give me that shit! Where is he?" I pulled out the twenty.

He sucked what was left of his fucked-up grill and snatched the money out of my hand.

After about ten minutes of driving through various lots, Slow pointed out the one Blue's ass was in. I saw his car parked in the lot, so I knew Slow was telling me the truth. "Which one?" I asked.

He pointed.

"He better be in here too." I flashed my gat at his ass.

"He is."

"Get on!" I snapped, and he rushed away. I wouldn't have been so fucked up to Slow but being that he was always near my pad there was no way he didn't know I was getting robbed. He had to have seen something.

I crept up to the steps and peered in the living room windows 'cause the chick had no blinds or curtains. All I saw was a kid sitting in the living room watching TV. The girl had to be about nine years old. Since her back was to me, I turned the knob. The living room door was even half-open.

When she saw me and my gun, her eyes widened.

I placed a finger to my lips.

She understood and nodded. But even if she did scream, I don't think the occupants in the room would have heard it.

I could hear a woman shouting, "Fuck me harder, daddy!"

A man answered, "Shut up, bitch!"

I glanced at the girl, feeling sorry for her. I pulled a twenty out of my pocket and tossed it at her. "Go get you something to eat, or whatever."

She didn't hesitate to take the money and rush out of the house.

Once she was gone, I walked toward the room. Without even waiting, I kicked the door open, putting a crack in it. I saw Blue's naked ass as he rode on top of some chick.

I rushed both of them, pulling Blue back by his braids and placing the gun at his temple.

"Bitch, what the fuck you doing in my house?" The girl jumped to her feet, buck-naked, like she wasn't afraid of the gun in my hand.

"Shut up, bitch!"

I reached over and smacked the shit out of her with my gun, knocking her out cold. Then I quickly placed the gun back at Blue's temple.

"Goldie, what the fuck is wrong with you?"

"Stop talking! I didn't say nobody in here could talk. Now, I got one question to ask you, and you better answer that shit."

"Man."

I bashed the gun into the side of his face, making him howl. "Muthafucka! I still ain't said that you could speak. I'm the only bitch that get to speak in here."

He nodded, and his hands shot up in surrender.

"All I want to know is this. And it is a simple yes or no. Was it Red?"

When he greeted me with silence, I slammed the gat down on his lips, making blood splatter.

He screamed like a bitch.

"Answer the fucking question, Blue! Was it Red that had your trifling ass rob me?"

He nodded his head quickly.

I released my hold on him, and he backed away from me.

As I turned to walk out of the room, from the corner of my eye, I saw him ball his fist and raise it in the air.

I spun around quickly and fired a shot, he jumped but he didn't get hit, I fired again. That shot was successful and had him spinning in a circle before falling to the ground.

He howled, "Why the fuck you shoot me?"

I ignored him and watched blood gush from one of his legs. You and Red ain't the baddest, muthafucka."

"You bitch!" He stayed on the floor rocking back and forth.

I walked out the house.

Chapter 41

Cha

"Mommy, turn that up!" Omari yelled.

"Okay."

We had been on the freeway for about twenty minutes. The radio was on the Disney station, and they were playing that darn song, "Umbrella" by Rihanna. Omari loved that dang song.

"*Umbrella, eh, eh, eh . . .*" he chirped.

I caught sight of my exit and got over quickly. I made a right onto the street and tried to make out the street on the paper. "Okay." I drove and scanned various streets until I found the right one. I damn near passed it up, so I broke quickly busted a u-turn and slipped between two lines that were not broken and made my left.

"Mama, the police behind you."

I took a breath as the lights flashed. They trailed probably because I'd made that quick turn in two lines that were not broken. Maybe it looked suspicious.

"Damn," I whispered.

I pulled over at the corner. My eyes spied the address on the curb, and I counted forward. The house was just three houses down.

The cop hopped out his car and scanned the license plate, as he approached my window. "Hello," he said.

"Hi, officer."

"Where you on your way to, ma'am?"

"To drop my friend's car off to get looked at and maybe fixed. Something is wrong with it."

He narrowed his eyes at me. "Ma'am, do you know what area you are in?"

I shrugged. Truthfully, I didn't.

He continued to stare at me. "So you're dropping a car off to be fixed?"

I nodded.

"Ma'am, you have to excuse my skepticism, but we've had a lot of drug trafficking in this neighborhood."

"I understand, but I'm not doing any of that. Plus, officer, I have my son in the car."

He used his flashlight and located my bag on the passenger side seat. Then he put them same lights on Omari, who covered his face with the back of his hand.

"Ma'am, you and your son need to step out of the car and place your hands on the hood, so I can do a routine search."

"Come on, Omari." I hopped out, and so did Omari. I held on to his hand.

"Put your hands on the car, ma'am. Your son as well."

"Offic—"

"Now!"

I did as he ordered and nodded at my son as well.

He was really tripping. He searched every crevice of the car, like I was a criminal. Then he went around to the trunk and popped it open.

Whatever ever he saw made him let out a loud long whistle.

I almost passed out when I saw him pull out bag after bag of what appeared to be pure cocaine. "Oh my God!"

"Ma'am, place your hands behind your head. Lace them!"

"Mama, what's happening?"

"Sssh," I told Omari.

I felt the pressure of the cuffs on my wrist and him chanting what I knew as my Miranda rights from watching so many episodes of *COPS*.

The next thing I know, I was sitting in the back of the squad car, and Omari was standing there with his hands on the hood of Red's car.

Chapter 42

Goldie

I was going to take care of that bitch. But, first, I had to go see my friend and make sure she was okay. Since I didn't give her that money, the hundred I'd pulled from my emergency fund was for her. I would report my school check missing, and once I got it again, I would break Cha off.

I pulled up to her lot and parked. When I got out of my car and made it to her steps, I saw her neighbor Tina pacing in a circle in her yard. My heart sank 'cause instantly I knew something was wrong.

When she saw me, she raced in my direction. "Goldie!"

I narrowed my eyes at her. "What? Where's Cha?"

"She called me from the police station 'cause she couldn't get in contact with you!"

"Police station?" My hands started shaking. I brought them up to my face.

"I don't know. I know Cha was going through it, with no food for her boy. All her utilities were shut off, and I didn't have any more to share, so I guess—"

"Tina! What is going on with Cha?"

"The police got her on drug trafficking! And they got Omari."

Chapter 43

Cha

They had me in a holding cell, where all I could think about was my son. And how I got myself into this.

Funny part was, if you'd asked me if I thought Red would set me up like this, I would have laughed. Who could or who would ever be that cruel?

Dear Lord, please make sure my baby is safe. And I'll accept any punishment for being stupid, but protect my son.

Unable to sleep, I cried until my eyes burned.

Chapter 44

Goldie

I didn't know where to turn, so I went to Rick, the only one I knew who had knowledge about the law. I hadn't seen or talked to him since he left the hospital that day. I found him at a desk typing something on a computer.

"Hi," I said. I bit my bottom lip and waited for him to turn me away.

"Hi, baby."

I was flooded with relief. "I really, really need you, Rick." Tears started shooting from my eyes.

Ten minutes later, he was hacking away on his computer. When he found Cha's info, he shook his head. "Whew!"

"What?"

"They found three kilos of cocaine on her."

"What does that carry?"

"Twenty years."

"What!"

"If she pleads guilty, they will reduce it to ten."

"My friend can't stay in jail for ten years. She has a son. A little boy!" I wanted to cry again. "Where is her son anyway?"

He made a phone call to Child Protective Services.

"Yes, this is Officer Green. I'm looking for a ward,

Omari Rapier. What placement is he located at?" Rick jotted something down.

I couldn't go see Cha unless I had some hope for her.

"He's at a foster home."

"Bullshit! I want him. My friend don't want to have anybody she don't know taking care of her son."

"All you have to do is call his social worker."

"And?"

"What they usually do is get consent from the parent, run a background on you, and if it comes back clean, he is all yours, babe."

I stopped listening after he said *background* and *clean*, since I had an assault on my record.

Seven Years Earlier

I was on the bus twiddling my thumbs. The urgency to pee wouldn't go away. I couldn't believe I was doing this shit. I thought of my boyfriend Daryl's words two days earlier.

"How the fuck could you let this happen?"

I sat at the kitchen table shocked at his reaction. I glanced at the steak and potatoes I had prepared, and the candles. I thought announcing my pregnancy would make him happy. He had a job. Plus, he was older than me. I was eighteen, and he was thirty. He was a truck driver and was gone for days at a time. With a baby not only did I have somebody else to love I had somebody to occupy me when he was gone.

"You not having that fucking baby!" he yelled and slammed out of our apartment.

Two days later, he gave me three hundred dollars, some bus tokens, and a brochure. "Don't come back to my crib with a baby in your stomach," he said. "That's not why I'm with you, to get fat and pregnant."

I swallowed my tears and walked out of the house.

The metro let me off right across from the clinic. As I crossed the street toward the clinic, located on Long Beach Boulevard, I glanced around embarrassed that anyone might see me. Various people lined the sidewalk, passing out flyers. They had a big-ass banner that said, ABORTION IS MURDER.

Then there were some homeless people huddled in a corner, and some peeps my age hanging out.

After I crossed the street, I noticed one person in particular wouldn't stop staring at me. She was my height, light-skin, freckles, had long red hair, and looked around the same age as me. She was leaning against the wall with two other dudes. I didn't have the energy to even question what she was looking at, so I dropped my head down and went inside.

After I checked in, I looked around to find somewhere to sit. The place was packed, and the only available seat was next to a chick that had an expression that said, "Bitch, I wish you would." On one side were the females who were expecting and coming in for their prenatal checkups. The other side was females terminating their pregnancies. Man I wish I could be on the other side.

Only one girl in the room gave me a friendly look. She looked distraught as well. When she caught me looking at her, she smiled. I smiled back and sat next to her.

"Nervous?" she asked me.

I nodded.

"Me too."

"I want to keep it," I said.

"Well, I don't."

Damn! Didn't every woman feel remorse about killing

a baby, whether they wanted it or not? She was cold. Maybe I shouldn't have sat next to her ass.

"It's a little hard to want to keep it when you were forced to have sex by more than one person so you don't know who the daddy is."

My eyes widened by how raw she was. *Damn!* Her situation was worse than mine.

I didn't know shit about this girl. Maybe she was lying, but looking in her eyes, I saw a lot of pain. "How old are you?" I asked her.

"I'm seventeen, but in another six months I'll be eighteen, and my pain will be all over. The next time I get pregnant, I'm hoping it will be created out of love."

A few tears slipped from her eyes.

That's how I met Cha.

During the wait, Cha broke down her situation, and I broke down mine. I was living with a man way older than I was and being wifey to him. Since I had run away from my grandma, I went from one man to another, but this one, I really loved. And she was forced to be wifey to a man and his two sons.

My heart started beating when they finally called my name. I was to go before Cha, who stayed in the waiting room and watched my stuff for me.

After they put one of them gowns on me and led me back to the surgery room, I took one look at the IV they were about to stick in my arm and leaped off the bed. I ran the fuck out of there. I wasn't killing my baby for nobody.

I ran out of the clinic. And when my boyfriend asked me whether or not I got the abortion. I threw his money back at him and yelled, "I'm, not killing my fucking baby!"

And the next time I went to that clinic I sat on the

other side with the other expectant mothers. And sure enough Cha showed up shortly after me with some girl I had never seen before, she was light skin with long thick red hair she had in a curly ponytail and a gang on freckles on her face.

Cha waved at me. I waved back.

The girl with her went to the booth and said loudly. "I need a muthafucking abortion."

"Well young lady there are many options."

"I'm not carrying this fucking baby."

"May I ask you why?" the lady said. She was the same person who I had spoken to my first time there. They almost try to talk you out of getting the abortion.

"'Cause I'm pregnant by a damn Gump."

"A Gump?" the lady looked confused.

"A fucking retard. I want this bastard out of me. And if you don't I'm gonna get rid of him the old fashion way by sticking a hanger up me."

That bitch was crazy.

"Red!" The girl Cha called her name.

She looked over at Cha then back to the lady. "What the fuck I need to do?"

The lady passed her a clipboard with papers on it. She went over and sat next to Cha.

I was surprised to see my boyfriend's car parked at the corner. And even more surprised when three chicks got out of it and rushed toward me. Before I could say anything one of them, a lady who appeared to be in her thirties, knocked me dead in my mouth. I looked at her confused then rage took over me but I couldn't get into a fight. I would hurt my baby.

"Bitch you had the nerve to get pregnant by my husband. Its not enough you fucking him huh?" she demanded.

Husband?

Before I could respond another woman snatched me up by my hair and the other girl was throwing punches, all while the "wife" walked around us in a circle. I yanked myself away and kept shoving them back to avoid them hitting my stomach. When they tried to shove my on my back I aimed my leg and kicked one bitch in her mouth. Then I jumped to my feet before the other one could throw another punch. I drilled her in her face with one hand and guarded my stomach with the other. But the bitches kept coming. I didn't have the man power to keep fighting both of them off.

I couldn't think of anyone else to scream for so I called Cha's name and prayed she heard me. My hair was yanked again and I was punched again. I twisted myself out feeling strands of my hair snap. I elbowed one bitch and swung on the other again getting her in the center of her chest. But in that moment I guess she caught me without my hand protecting my stomach because before I could dodge her, the wife jabbed my stomach with all her might with something so hard that it felt like steel. The pain was so intense I dropped to my knees as a series of cramps hit my abdomen.

"Bitch I'm gonna beat that fucking baby out of you!"

I fell to the ground on my side and the more seconds that flew by the more pain I felt. It was almost like it paralyzed me. But that didn't stop the assault. I was kicked in the head, received more punches in my stomach and even felt spit hit my face.

I curled up in a ball unable to get up or defend myself any longer.

That's when Cha and her friend came flying our way.

"Why you getting in that shit?" I heard Red ask loudly.

"Just help me!" Cha told her.

That's when I heard, "Ya'll old bitches need to leave her the fuck alone." That was Red.

They ignored her and kept assaulting me. That's when Cha and Red jumped in and were in a full fledge fight with the bitches while I stayed on the concrete. I watched the wife back up while her two accomplices were fighting Red and Cha.Thats when I saw it, blood leaking between my legs onto the concrete.

The wife saw it too. So she smiled.

I spied what she had assuated me with. A crowbar. It was inches from where I lay. I rolled over and grabbed it and before she could stop me, I rushed toward the car she arrived in and I went to work on it. I busted out all the windows and put a series of dents all over the muthafucka.

She screamed for me to stop. But that's when I went after that bitch. My walk was slow due to the pain but I was on her. She ran around to the back of the car. I followed, then she ran to the other side. I felt dizzy and continued to cramp but I wasn't going to put that tool down until I fucked her up with it. She ran around the car back to where the fighting continued. She backed up and starting jogging backward, I guess she wanted to keep her eyes on me for fear I would strike her in her back but she ended up tripping over her own feet and falling to the ground. That was my chance to get that bitch. "Please don't," she begged holding both her hands up in surrender. But I didn't give a fuck. She didn't give a fuck about my baby who didn't do anything to her. Lets just say that I did know that Daryl was married, which I didn't, but even if I did, my baby still was innocent and she took its life 'cause her husband was fucking me? I raised the crow bar above my head about to end this bitch's world when I heard, "Drop your fucking weapon!"

The only thing good out of that whole ordeal was meeting Cha and Red, because we'd been tight ever since that day. Who knew Red would do this?

"What, baby?"

I turned back to Rick. "I have something on my record. I'm sorry."

He closed his eyes. "It's okay, baby. But what you have to understand is, with a record, you won't be able to have custody, temporary or permanent, of Omari."

Tears slipped from my eyes.

"You technically won't be able to see Cha either."

"I have to see her."

He knew what I was thinking. I was asking him to do something illegal.

"You know what you asking me to do?"

I nodded.

Chapter 45

Cha

Nothing felt better. I kept waking up to the same horrible reality, grooming with the rest of the inmates, eating the dull breakfast with dull stares, sexual stares, pity stares, and hateful stares so scary I went on in my cell instead of going to church which is what I needed more than anything this Sunday. I had been here for a week, got into two fights, been jumped and even raped by one of the guards. I had developed the habit of sleeping the day and night away. But I couldn't sleep tomorrow away because I had court and today, finally today, I had a visit. When the guard handed me my visiting slip I looked at it curiously because I did not recognize the names on it. So I went on ahead and stood in the line with the other inmates and surprise, ease and joy was what I felt when I saw Goldie's face staring back at me. She was seated next to a dude that I did not recognize at first. But upon closer inspection I did. It was the officer from the Carmelitos, Rick.

I took a seat and snatched up the phone.

"How are you?" Goldie asked me.

I offered a smile and nodded to Rick.

"How you get that black eye?" Goldie looked around at the other inmates across from her with a mean expression.

"Sucker punch."

Goldie's face went from agitated to furious in a matter of seconds. I knew she had no problem at all standing up and cursing out these inmates in here. Rick placed his hand over hers, and she took a deep breath.

"Any word on Omari?" I asked.

Goldie bit her bottom lip. "They won't let me see him, Cha."

I nodded and rubbed my hands together. "I just wish I knew he was okay."

"I checked out the place he's at."

"Where is he?"

"Olive Road."

"Oh God! A group home? Goldie, you know how I feel about that."

"I know, Cha, but now we have to focus on getting you out of here." Goldie nodded.

"Goldie, I promise you on a stack of bibles that I truly didn't know that those drugs were there. I needed money, and I hadn't heard from you."

"I–"

"No. Don't explain. I know you had to have a good reason for not coming. And it's not your responsibility, me and Omari. Red told me she would give me the money she owed me plus an extra hundred. She even said sorry about what happened with the three-way."

Rick's eyes widened and he broke into a coughing fit.

"All she said I had to do was drive her car to that house so they could check out the timing belt. Well, I guess cops were patrolling that area. It don't matter what I say or do. I was driving the car with the stuff in it. Unless Red comes in and says that it's her stuff, I'm going down for it.

Goldie was enraged at the mention of Red's name. "That dirty, low-down bitch. I—"

"I know you said not to fuck with her, but I was desperate. The lights and phone were off. We had no food. Funny part was, that day I was doing a lot of thinking about what we talked about that day we beat up the repo man."

Rick shot Goldie a look, and she gave him a tight smile.

"I realized, if Omari was so important to me, then I couldn't let my old boss or that doctor win. Man, was I pumped up. I figured if I could get one job, then I could always get another. At that moment, losing my welfare didn't mean anything to me. I was almost happy because it motivated me further. Then this happened. I can kiss my dreams good-bye."

"No, you not!" Goldie yelled.

"Goldie, you know what charge I'm facing?"

"Yes. Rick said you should plead guilty. It carries ten years, and you'd probably serve half of that, since you have no record."

"What? Five years? Goldie, I can't be away from my baby for five years." I started crying again. "Goldie, you know what happened to me in that place?"

"I know, baby, but—"

"I'm not going to be able to function, live my life, knowing he can't be near me, that I can't protect him." I sobbed uncontrollably.

Goldie was now crying.

"Forget that, Goldie. I tell you, I'd rather die. I'm not gonna live on this earth and be separated from him. I would never feel right. It would be like I'm giving him away." I blew

Goldie a kiss and hung up the phone. I placed my right hand over my heart to tell her I love her.

Then I rose up from my seat and kept on walking, ignoring the tapping on the window.

Chapter 46

Goldie

I shoved a plate of bacon, scrambled eggs, hash browns, and toast away from me. I saw Cha's face again. Her face, her eyes kept on haunting me. My appetite ain't been the same since I found out she was in that square box called hell.

My body didn't feel right either, nor could I keep my head from aching. Or my stomach from cramping. Every other hour I had to shit. I was stressin' about Cha.

"Try to eat a little, baby." Rick placed my plate back in front of me.

I gave him a half-smile. We were in the cafeteria at the courthouse waiting for Cha's hearing. And I just wanted to get this shit over with. I wanted to know that my friend, after all of this, would be okay, but honestly not feeling that she would and scared to mouth it.

I gnawed on my last long nail out of ten.

Rick sipped his coffee. When he saw I went to biting my last nail down to a nub then to tapping restlessly on the table, he placed both of his hands over mine.

I dropped my eyes and shook my head. "What time is it?"

"Eight fifteen. Come on."

He stood and helped me out of my seat, and we walked into the courtroom.

Ten minutes after we sat down, two guards brought a shackled Cha in the room. My heart caved into my chest when I saw her. She struggled to walk in the shackles around her ankles and steadied herself by holding her handcuffed hands in front of her.

I closed my eyes and said a quick prayer. *God, please help and bless my friend. God, give her the chance to be with her son, to raise him and be happy.* Then I held Rick's hand. He pulled it to his lips and kissed it. Then he squeezed it tight.

Cha glanced my way quickly. She gave me that pretty smile of hers.

I smiled back and winked, even though inside I was crumbling. But if she could hold it together, I could too.

The judge banged his gavel and said loudly, as if annoyed he was even there, "Are we ready to start?"

The guards stood next to my friend like she was a damn criminal.

"Why do they have to treat her like that?" I asked Rick.

"Relax, baby."

The more I sat there and listened to that bullshit, the more I wanted to flip a table over. They talked about my friend like she wasn't shit. It was bull. The prosecutor ripped my friend to shreds.

"Your Honor, Ms. Rapier is an unfit mother fully prepared to flood our streets with kilos of crack cocaine. Yes, she is beautiful. She looks sweet. But she is a criminal who indulges as well. Your Honor, she tested positive for marijuana, ecstasy, and cocaine."

My eyes as well as Cha's eyes popped open.

"On December twenty-second, two thousand eight, at nine P.M., Chandria Rapier was driving a car that she was fully aware had four kilos of cocaine in the trunk. She was also fully aware of the location she was taking it to: A crack house. She, I repeat, was prepared to flood this neighborhood with drugs. Drugs that men women and kids use. Drugs that kill, and increase crime. She was willing to do it all with her five-year-old son in the car with her. We ask for the minimum sentence of twenty years."

I jumped at those last words. I wanted to kill that bitch, Red. *Maybe I would, whether Cha gets off or not.*

Without even looking at Cha, the judge said, "Stand."

Cha did, tears sliding off her face.

"How do you plead?" He flipped through a file.

"Guilty, your Honor."

"Your Honor, my client has never been in trouble. She simply lost her way. She is a victim of abuse and has been in group homes all her life."

The judge stared at Cha and narrowed his eyes at her. "It says here you have never been arrested."

"No, sir."

"So why would a mother put herself in such a risky situation?" He bit the tip of one side of his glasses.

Cha shrugged. "I just made a mistake, Your Honor."

"Your Honor, Chandria realizes that she made a huge mistake. She had no food, her lights were off, and she simply wanted to feed her son. The opportunity came, and she took it in desperation. My client wants nothing more than to put this behind her, get a job, go back to school, and raise her son."

The judge listened. It gave me hope. Maybe they would let my friend off.

"Let me hear it from her, counsel."

Cha cleared her throat. "Your Honor, my son is the most important thing to me. He has always been. I want to

give him what I never had. My mama gave birth to me in an alley. She wrapped me in newspaper and placed me in a dumpster. I been in group homes ever since. I been abused sexually
since I was ten. I don't want my son to go through that. I want
to heal myself so that I can be all that I possibly can for him.
I want to go back to school, be a pre-school teacher. I want
to get off in time to help my son with his homework. I want
to make real home-cooked meals, teach him about life, how
to treat a woman. Your Honor, I can't do that in here. All
my being in here will do is strengthen the possibility of him
standing before you eight years from now."

The judge stared at Cha for a long time.

"Plea," he said to the district attorney.

"Your Honor, we ask for at most one year and three
years probation." The evil-ass DA looked pissed that he
couldn't stick the twenty years to Cha.

Evil bastard!

"That sounds possible."

I smiled and breathed deeply.

"We will adjourn for lunch." He banged the gavel.

Cha looked back at me and smiled, and I blew her a
kiss.

Now I was able to eat something. I rose and walked
hand in hand with Rick back to the cafeteria. I ordered a
double cheeseburger, fries, and a Coke and Rick ordered a
chicken fajita platter.

Once we sat down, I attacked my burger. Rick watched
me and laughed.

"A year ain't shit! Cha can do that." I tossed a fry in
my mouth. "The only concern would be Omari. I can't get
him, so he would still be in a foster home for a year."

"Don't worry, Goldie," Rick said, spooning some chicken and peppers into a flour tortilla. "You prayed, so leave the worrying to God. Things are going to work out. Your friend's record is clear, and this judge has a natural sympathy for single parents."

"Yeah, you right." I grabbed his fork and started spooning some of his chicken into my mouth. I was starving.

Thirty minutes later we were back in the courtroom. This time we were able to sit in the second row.

Cha walked back in escorted by two guards again.

The judge walked out slowly. He shifted the papers in his hands. Then he took a deep breath. He banged his gavel. "Will the defendant stand."

Cha rose alongside her public defender.

"I have a habit of having a soft spot for single parents and past wards of the court. My mother was a single parent and she had six of us. She did everything she could to take care of us. And I have no doubt that she would have done *anything* to ensure our survival. So, young lady, I sympathize with you because my mother could have very well been you. But, unfortunately, due to the amount of the drugs, you stepped over into federal law, and I have no choice but to give you the minimum sentence of twenty years in a federal prison."

"What?" I screamed.

He grabbed his gavel but made no move to slam it.

I started bawling. I made a move to rush toward Cha, but Rick held me in place. I was shaking and sobbing, shaking my head. This had to be a dream.

Cha almost fell, but the guards held her up. One guard walked in front of her to open the mini-door for them to pass.

"Cha," I called.

She gave me one fleeting glance, and while the other guard walked behind her, she rushed forward and snatched the gun from the guard who was standing with his back to her. Before they could even make a move to get it from her, she pointed it at her temple and fired.

Chapter 47

Goldie

I probably should have given myself a little more time to grieve over Cha's death. But the more I cried the angrier I got because my friend was dead and this bitch was still living.

I found her ass seated at a table with all dudes at To-bos.

She tipped her glass back and eyed me over the lid. "What it do, shorty?" She smiled.

I took a deep, deep breath, fury seeping into me. "Do you know what the fuck you did?"

She downed another glass of her Hypnotiq like she didn't have a care in the world, when my heart was still doing somersaults for Cha.

"Cha, in case you didn't know, is dead, Red! She killed herself."

She didn't blink.

"She killed herself because she knew she wouldn't be able to be with her son."

"Okay, and what the fuck you want me to do? I'm down with Red and Red only. You and her knew that. Cha was down to make the money so you accept the consequences that come with it. So don't come in here fucking up my high with talk about her silly ass and her little pig."

That's when I rushed her. I lunged over the table and leaped on top of her ass so she flew back, and I flew right with her. I started throwing punches and slaps, whatever I could do to hurt that bitch. Her swings hit the air, and every time she swung, I jabbed her in her face.

I finally took one of my hands and gripped it around her throat and kept punching her until her face started puffing out and her lip became busted. She took her fingers and dug her nails into my face.

"Bitch, you always fight dirty!"

I used the only thing I had. My head.

Blood filled, and instantly spilled from her nose. She cupped it in both of her hands and threw it in my face, and I quickly closed my eyes.

Meanwhile, a crowd formed around us, but I didn't care. I was finding any and everything I could use against this bitch—filled bottles of drink, empty bottles—and bashing her in the head, wherever I possibly could. I was fucking the bitch up.

She stood to her feet and lunged toward me, and I went down with the weight of her body, so she was over me. I had my knee in her pussy and continued slapping her left and right until her face was as flush red as the blood oozing from her broken nose.

That's when she started strangling me.

I balled my fist and punched her in the nose again, and she flew backward. That's when I went crazy busting her in the head with whatever I could put my hands on. I threw both my shoes and even a chair at her.

She gave up trying to beat me and tried to get away by crawling on her knees. Guess she was too weak to walk.

I kept socking and kicking until she was coughing and

spitting up blood. Then I realized the crowd was cheering for me.

When she finally collapsed on her side, I used my feet to kick her flat on her back. In that moment, with a gash on her forehead, a broken nose that she couldn't even breathe out of, and a fucked-up mouth, she actually smiled. The bitch smiled.

I pulled out my gat and aimed it in her fucked-up face, and damned if I didn't want to take that steel and end her life with it. But then I thought about it. I would be just like her. 'Cause, yeah, Cha pulled the trigger on herself, but in my mind Red would always be the killer.

"You a black-hearted bitch!" I yelled. "I wish you a lifetime of misery and pain!" I grabbed a broken bottle lying next to my feet and slashed the side of her face. "

She grabbed her bloodied face and made a move to attack, but something behind me had her shook. But I wasn't going to turn my back and let the bitch get me. Then I heard thundering behind me, and somebody shoved me out of the way.

I had a slew of curse words on my lips. I held my tongue, though, when I realized four chicks that looked like hoes rushed Red and started beating her with fists and feet. One girl had a bat and started fucking her up.

My eyes bucked when, all of a sudden, I heard the screams of what sounded like a little girl saying, "No, Mommy! I know I'm a monkey! I'm a dirty nigger. Don't beat me anymore!"

I shook my head and zeroed in on where the words were coming from. They were coming from Red.

One of the hoes, the one with the bat, said, "Shut up, bitch! You wasn't pleading when you was stealing Damu's hoes away!" She swiped her in the head with the bat.

Then one of the hoes put her hand on it and said, "No, don't kill her. Daddy said he is gonna put her on the track to make up the money she lost him. He know where to find her when it's time."

After that, the beating stopped, and all the hoes smoothly walked away.

I stared at this girl I once considered to be my girl. Me, her, and Cha were as thick as thieves ever since that day I met her and Cha at the abortion clinic. I always wanted to ask Red why she chose to help me instead of Daryl, but I figured it was about a girl helping out another girl. But knowing who the girl is now, it had to be that she thought she would benefit in some way by helping me.

And she did.

When we were all cool, she had friends that would never back down, as far as she was concerned. Me and Cha would always protect her.

Those days were long over. I didn't know the person lying in that pool of blood anymore. Even if her heart continued to beat, she was pretty much dead to me, just walking death.

So I said a quick prayer for her, took a deep breath, and headed toward the door.

"You should have killed that bitch!" someone shouted.

I ignored her.

"You mean this dirty ho gonna walk the streets after all the dirt she has done? Turning them poor girls into hoes?"

I shrugged to the question. Made my way to the exit slowly. My whole body was sore. I hadn't fucked anybody up in a long time.

As soon as my hand reached for the door, it was shoved open so hard that, if I hadn't stepped back, my ass would have got smacked in the face with it.

Two dudes rushed through and another on crutches followed, and despite him keeping his head down, I recognized one of them was Blue. He was able to grab Red's ponytail and help the other two guys drag her limp body outside.

The crowd followed behind them, and I did too, curious as to what they were doing, 'cause Blue was her boy.

One of the three said, "Red, you lost three kilos of cocaine. You thought you could walk the streets, bitch?"

"Get off of me! That shit wasn't my fault. I already squared it away with Rock. He said it's cool." When she spied me she had that look on her face from back in the day where she just knew I was going to get her out of this situation.

Not this time or any other for that matter. I just watched in silence as Red struggled against them, but they managed to shove her in her car.

One of them used his foot to keep her lay back in the front seat. "Stay down!" He punched her in her face, knocking her out cold. That's when I recognized him. It was Don.

The other guy pulled out a bottle of gasoline and dumped it all over her until she was soaked.

Next, Blue took his lighter, flicked it on, and tossed it inside of the car. Like paper, she instantly went up in flames.

They kicked the doors closed, and while my friend burned up inside. They calmly walked away.

Chapter 48

Goldie

When you lose someone you truly loved and then hated, you feel like a damn fool because at one time you loved them just as much as you hated them, and perhaps you still did. Shit. Sentiments such as these made me feel utterly conflicted.

Cha was dead. My poor friend had given up hope. How could I, or anyone else for that damn matter, blame her? Hell, I would be a walking train wreck if I was her. Hell, I'd probably walk into a fucking train.

It had been officially three weeks since Cha's and Red's deaths. I, like a dumb ass, did the worst thing I could have possibly done. But to me at the time it was the best thing.

I shut Rick out. Well, first, I blamed him for Cha's death. I thought back to the day I closed my heart to him.

"Had you not told her to plead guilty, this shit wouldn't have happened!" I slapped him and beat him in the chest and sobbed hard. "I hate you, Rick!"

He let me use him as a punching bag though, so I kept on biting him and hitting him until my fingers were numb.

"Get the fuck out, Rick!"

"Goldie."

"Get out!"

He stood with his hands on his hips and watched me act a damn fool, like he was waiting for me to take back what I told him. But I had no intention to. So he walked out quietly. In these past three weeks I realized I needed Rick more than ever. Pride fucked that up. He had been calling me non-stop, but I refused to answer.

I forced myself to get up today. Although it was three weeks past Christmas I went to Toys 'R' Us to buy Omari some things. I was pretty sure they wouldn't let me see Omari, but I was sure they would let me drop some gifts off to them.

I had gone in my savings, so I had enough. I threw a Wii, some games, a leap frog, some books, and an MP3 player in the basket. Once I paid for them, I tossed them in the back of my car and set out for the home Rick told me he was at.

I wish I could see him, I thought, as I got out of my car lugging the bags.

A woman who appeared to be in her mid-thirties opened the door. "May I help you?" she asked me.

I didn't even trip when she didn't invite me inside. "Hi," I said after clearing my throat. "I am a friend of Omari's mother."

"Okay."

"I know I'm not allowed to see him. I just came to drop off some gifts to him."

"What is the kid's name again?"

"Omari Rapier, ma'am."

"Hmmm." She looked puzzled for a moment. "Were you not informed?" Then she waved a hand before I could answer again. "Oh, yes, you're not next of kin or any blood relation, so they wouldn't tell you. Omari was adopted. He left two days ago."

Tears instantly clouded my vision. I put one of my shaking hands to my chest. Now I'd never see him. My friend was probably tossing around in her grave.

"Are you okay?"

I shook my head because I couldn't get any words out.

She looked behind her, stepped out on the steps, and closed the door to the house. "Are you going to be okay, honey?"

I nodded, wiping my tears off my face and handing her the bags. "I'm sure you could put these to use, ma'am." I walked down the steps of the house and into the direction of my car.

"Young lady!"

I turned around and saw the woman chasing after me, out of breath. Once she reached me, she looked back at the house then back to me.

"I shouldn't be saying this. I could get written up, but being that you concerned and all, Omari's gonna be just fine. There was a very nice gentleman who adopted little Omari." She put her arm on my shoulder like we were old friends. "And, honey chile, was he handsome. You should have seen all these buck-eyed heiffas trying to get his attention, but he wasn't going for none of it. That man sure knew how to wear a uniform." She lowered her voice, saying, "If I wasn't worried I would get written up, I would have told him he could arrest me any time!"

I froze as she burst into laughter.

"He was a what?"

"An officer. And finer than—"

I rushed up to my car unlocked it, dove in, started the ignition, and sped away.

I sped down the highway like crazy to Rick's house.

When I got there, I got out and ran up to the steps

and knocked like crazy. His car was there, but no one answered the door. I tried to call him on his cell phone, but it
went straight to voice mail.

I got into my car about to turn the ignition when I
saw a squad car turn down the block. I saw Rick driving. It
had to be.

I jumped out of my car as his car came to a stop alongside mine. I watched as he made a move to open the back seat.
Tears poured from my eyes, and I looked up to the sky when I
saw little Omari hop out of the back seat of the car.

Chapter 49

Goldie

One Year Later

"Shit!"

The professor was boring the fuck out of me. And, to tell the truth, creative writing wasn't my thing. I just wished this shit would be over with.

I was so into my own annoyance, it took a while before I noticed the entire class had turned around to look at me.

My professor was staring at me also because of my outburst. "Goldie, is there a problem?"

"Naw. I'm cool."

A couple of students snickered at me.

"But I wish muthafuckas would stop laughing! I'm trying to concentrate on the lecture."

Professor Roquefort looked like she didn't know what to do with my ghetto ass. She was probably going to kick me out for good. I didn't care. It wasn't like I was doing good in her class anyway. Every paper I did, she always gave me a grade no higher than a C. It was this class and my other class, "Shakespeare" that got on my muthafucking nerves. That crazy lady was so fucking obsessed with Shakespeare, you would have thought she was fucking him. Why, oh why, did I decide to be an English teacher?

I stared at the clock and breathed a sigh of relief because it was time to go.

"All right. You can come and pick up your papers off the desk," the professor said, obviously giving up on me.

I sat in my seat and waited for all the traffic from students getting their papers to die down.

Then there was one other person, this white chick, the one who snickered at me. She looked at me when I stood behind her.

I gave her a mean look and whispered, "Laugh now, bitch," and she rushed away.

I went through the remaining stack of papers that must have been students who didn't show up for class today. "Ain't this some shit!" I said out loud.

The teacher looked at me from her desk. "Goldie, can you come here please."

I took a deep breath and approached her.

"Is something wrong?" her bubble-eyed ass asked.

"Yeah. Out of all the people in here, my paper ain't in the stack."

She smiled and opened a manila folder on her desk. "I have a good idea why." She pulled my paper out and handed it to me.

My eyes got buck when I saw the red A+ written on the paper.

"That was an excellent paper. Goldie, you are a good student and intelligent, but the difference in this paper from the others was the personal immersion. That's what creative writing is about, digging into yourself. You mastered that here."

"Thank you, Miss."

She nodded. "Goldie, I was very touched by your story

about your friend, Chandria. The reason I added it in my folder and not in the stack was that I was going to ask if I could include it in my lecture for a convention I am attending at Berkeley this weekend."

"What?" I almost didn't hear her. *She wanted to use my paper?*

"You heard me. I want to use it in my presentation. The paper is so touching about your friend, and the way you wrote it was amazing. But I need your permission."

I smiled and placed the paper back in her hands, my eyes watering.

Then I turned and rushed out of the classroom to share the news with two important people.

I speed-walked to the parking lot. *Who would have known my work would be presented at Berkley? What?*

I saw Rick and Omari parked in his squad car. I walked over to them to share the good news. Little Omari was sitting in the squad car with ice cream all over him.

"Where is mine?"

Omari giggled and passed a container of banana nut ice cream to me and a plastic spoon.

"Baby, guess what?" I said to Rick, who was licking on his own cone.

He pulled me in his arms and kissed me. "What, baby?"

I blushed as chicks walked by, catching sight of me and my officer. Ha! "My professor wanted to use one of my stories in a lecture."

"That's good, baby. Which one?"

"The one about Chandria." I scooped some ice cream out of the cup and dipped the spoon in my mouth.

I bit down on something hard and said out loud,

"Shit!" Instantly I thought I had bit into a rat head, like the lady did while eating at some food establishment years ago. I gagged, screaming, "Baby! Baby!"

"What's wrong, auntie?" Omari asked.

I curved a finger and fearfully swept whatever it was out of my mouth. I looked down at a ring. I dropped the ice cream, looked again, and there it was, sparkling back at me.

I looked at Rick, who dropped to his knees instantly.

Before he could get the question out, I slipped the ring on my finger and ran around the parking lot like a mad woman.